FINDING HOME

FINDING SERIES #1

SLOANE KENNEDY

CONTENTS

Finding Home is a work of fiction. Names, characters, businesses, places, events and incidents are either the products of the author's imagination or used in a fictitious manner. Any resemblance to actual persons, living or dead, or actual events is purely coincidental.

Copyright © 2015 by Sloane Kennedy

Published in the United States by Sloane Kennedy

Cover Images: © 2013 Mary Chronis, VJ Dunraven Productions & PeriodImages.com

Cover Design: © Jay Aheer, Simply Defined Art

ISBN-13:
978-1541060333

ISBN-10:
1541060334

FINDING HOME

Sloane Kennedy

ACKNOWLEDGMENTS

A big thank you to Stephanie for being such an amazing Beta Reader!

SERIES READING ORDER

All of my series cross over with one another so I've provided a couple of recommended reading orders for you. If you want to start with the Protectors books, use the first list. If you want to follow the books according to timing, use the second list. Note that you can skip any of the books (including M/F) as each was written to be a standalone story.

Note that some books may not be readily available on all retail sites

Recommended Reading Order (Use this list if you want to start with "The Protectors" series)
1. Absolution (m/m/m) (The Protectors, #1)
2. Salvation (m/m) (The Protectors, #2)
3. Retribution (m/m) (The Protectors, #3)
4. Gabriel's Rule (m/f) (The Escort Series, #1)
5. Shane's Fall (m/f) (The Escort Series, #2)
6. Logan's Need (m/m) (The Escort Series, #3)
7. Finding Home (m/m/m) (Finding Series, #1)
8. Finding Trust (m/m) (Finding Series, #2)

9. Loving Vin (m/f) (Barretti Security Series, #1)
10. Redeeming Rafe (m/m) (Barretti Security Series, #2)
11. Saving Ren (m/m/m) (Barretti Security Series, #3)
12. Freeing Zane (m/m) (Barretti Security Series, #4)
13. Finding Peace (m/m) (Finding Series, #3)
14. Finding Forgiveness (m/m) (Finding Series, #4)
15. Forsaken (m/m) (The Protectors, #4)
16. Vengeance (m/m/m) (The Protectors, #5)
17. A Protectors Family Christmas (The Protectors, #5.5)
18. Atonement (m/m) (The Protectors, #6)
19. Revelation (m/m) (The Protectors, #7)
20. Redemption (m/m) (The Protectors, #8)
21. Finding Hope (m/m/m) (Finding Series, #5)
22. Defiance (m/m) (The Protectors #9)

Recommended Reading Order (Use this list if you want to follow according to timing)
1. Gabriel's Rule (m/f) (The Escort Series, #1)
2. Shane's Fall (m/f) (The Escort Series, #2)
3. Logan's Need (m/m) (The Escort Series, #3)
4. Finding Home (m/m/m) (Finding Series, #1)
5. Finding Trust (m/m) (Finding Series, #2)
6. Loving Vin (m/f) (Barretti Security Series, #1)
7. Redeeming Rafe (m/m) (Barretti Security Series, #2)
8. Saving Ren (m/m/m) (Barretti Security Series, #3)
9. Freeing Zane (m/m) (Barretti Security Series, #4)
10. Finding Peace (m/m) (Finding Series, #3)
11. Finding Forgiveness (m/m) (Finding Series, #4)
12. Absolution (m/m/m) (The Protectors, #1)
13. Salvation (m/m) (The Protectors, #2)
14. Retribution (m/m) (The Protectors, #3)
15. Forsaken (m/m) (The Protectors, #4)
16. Vengeance (m/m/m) (The Protectors, #5)
17. A Protectors Family Christmas (The Protectors, #5.5)

SERIES CROSSOVER CHART

Protectors/Barrettis/Finding Crossover Chart

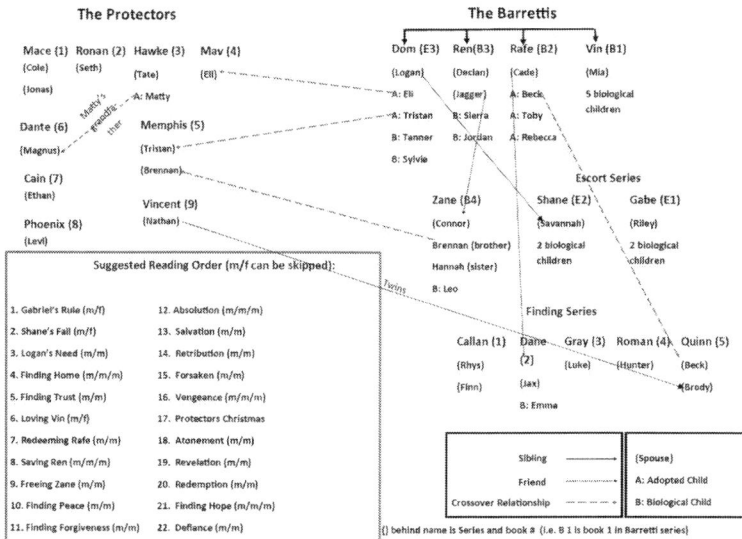

The Protectors

Mace (1)   Ronan (2)   Hawke (3)   Mav (4)

{Cole}   {Seth}   {Tate}   {Eli}

{Jonas}

Dante (6)   Memphis (5)

{Magnus}   {Tristan}

                         {Brennan}

Cain (7)

{Ethan}

                         Vincent (9)

Phoenix (8)   {Nathan}

{Levi}

The Barrettis

Dom {E3}   Ren{B3}   Rafe {B2}   Vin {B1}

{Logan}   {Declan}   {Cade}   {Mia}

A: Eli   {Jagger}   A: Beck   5 biological

A: Tristan B: Sierra A: Toby   children

B: Tanner B: Jordan A: Rebecca

           B: Sylvie

Zane {B4}

{Connor}

Brennan {brother}

Hannah {sister}

B: Leo

Escort Series

Shane {E2}   Gabe {E1}

{Savannah}   {Riley}

2 biological 2 biological
children   children

Finding Series

Callan (1)   Dane   Gray (3)   Roman (4)   Quinn (5)

{Rhys}   {2}   {Luke}   {Hunter}   {Beck}

{Finn}   {Jax}

             B: Emma

Matty's grandfather

Twin

Brody

Suggested Reading Order (m/f can be skipped):

1. Gabriel's Rule (m/f)	12. Absolution (m/m/m)
2. Shane's Fall (m/f)	13. Salvation (m/m)
3. Logan's Need (m/m)	14. Retribution (m/m)
4. Finding Home (m/m/m)	15. Forsaken (m/m)
5. Finding Trust (m/m)	16. Vengeance (m/m/m)
6. Loving Vin (m/f)	17. Protectors Christmas
7. Redeeming Rafe (m/m/m)	18. Atonement (m/m)
8. Saving Ren (m/m/m)	19. Revelation (m/m)
9. Freeing Zane (m/m)	20. Redemption (m/m)
10. Finding Peace (m/m)	21. Finding Hope (m/m/m)
11. Finding Forgiveness (m/m)	22. Defiance (m/m)

Sibling ————	{Spouse}
Friend ·············	A: Adopted Child
Crossover Relationship – – – –	B: Biological Child

{} behind name is Series and book # (i.e. B 1 is book 1 in Barretti series)

TRIGGER WARNING

Listed below are the trigger warnings for this book. Reading them may cause spoilers:

This book contains references to sexual assault.

CHAPTER 1

*R*hys Tellar stared at the iron arch above him and grimaced. A ranch in the heart of Bumfuck, Montana. This was where honesty and playing by the rules had gotten him – a dry, dusty piece of shit land that sat in the shadow of the Rocky Mountain range. He didn't see any cows, but he sure as hell could smell them as the winds shifted and a hot, stifling gust blew more grit onto his sweat soaked skin. The guy he'd hitched a ride with had told him the ranch sat a mile up past the entrance. He hoped to God that the rusty piece of metal that hung above his head with the initials CB on it was a sign that a cold shower and hot meal were in his near future. Fuck, they didn't even need to happen in that order.

He cursed his parole officer for the hundredth time as he began the long trek up the dirt road. Frank Pettit had sworn this place would be more receptive to hiring an ex-con without a lot of questions, though he wasn't sure what that said about the man running the place. If the guy he'd hitched with was right, the owner of the CB Bar Ranch was a major prick who'd alienated most of the little town of Dare and would be as likely to greet a newcomer with a shotgun as a handshake.

But it wasn't like Rhys had a lot of options. He'd blown through three jobs already in the six weeks he'd been out of prison, and it was only the fact that he and Frank had a previous personal relationship that had made it possible for him to even leave the state of Illinois to serve his parole. Being a former cop hadn't done him any favors when it came to the Parole Board, but Frank's reputation had been a game changer and the older man had called in every favor to get Rhys out of the state. Now if Rhys could just get his temper under control long enough to get a job in the exciting world of ranching, maybe he could start to get his life back on track. He just needed to get through six months in this hell hole and then he'd be in the free and clear and the first thing he'd do would be get his ass back to Chicago and settle some old scores.

Rhys hefted his duffle bag over his shoulder, ignoring the way his jeans were starting to stick in all the wrong places. Hearing the sound of an engine behind him, he turned to see an old, beat up, 70's era red pick-up truck bouncing its way up the road. He couldn't make out the driver, but wanted to shout for joy as the truck meandered to a crawl and then finally stopped next to him. The passenger window was open - a sure sign that air conditioning was probably too much to ask for – so he leaned in and wiped the sweat from his brow with the sleeve of his shirt.

"Hey-" he began, but then came to a stuttering halt when he saw the vision sitting in the driver's seat. Tousled blonde hair streaked with darker strands of gold, blue eyes, firm lips – and young...way too fucking young.

"Hi," said the young man, clearly unaware of how Rhys was internally drooling. "You need a lift up to the ranch?"

Rhys nodded, not quite trusting his tongue yet, especially since it had a mind of its own and wanted nothing more than to explore the lean, smooth column of the guy's throat.

"Hop in," he said with a smile. A good ole country boy. Rhys tossed his bag in the bed of the truck before climbing in next to the guy.

"I'm Finn," the guy offered as he held out his hand.

Rhys took it and held it for a little longer than necessary, enjoying the sparks prickling where their skin met. Finn seemed to notice it

2

too because his lips parted just slightly and a whisper of air escaped his lips before he pulled free.

"Rhys Tellar," Rhys said, hiding a knowing smile. If the kid wasn't gay, he was definitely curious and that had Rhys' dick taking notice. He quickly amended his previous list about wanting food and a cold shower. Finn's perfect mouth wrapped around Rhys' cock jumped to the top of the list. Finn fiddled with putting the truck in gear and Rhys shifted to try to buy himself some more room in his jeans.

"What brings you to the CB Bar, Rhys?" Finn asked nervously as he pressed the gas and the truck lurched forward. God, the kid's nerves turned Rhys on even more because he knew how receptive that would make the younger man.

"Job, hopefully," Rhys answered, his eyes scanning Finn, taking in the cowboy shirt, faded, worn jeans and cowboy boots. There was even a fucking cowboy hat on the seat between them. A cliché, but a hot one that Rhys couldn't wait to indulge in. "You work here?" Rhys asked.

Finn nodded and Rhys didn't miss the look of pride pass over the other man's features. "Going on six years now."

That made the kid well above the age to consent, Rhys thought to himself happily. He stretched his arm out across the back of the seat bench and wondered if Finn's hair was as soft as it looked. Would he cry out when Rhys held it as he fucked him from behind?

"So you're a real live cowboy," Rhys drawled.

Finn chuckled and said, "I guess so."

"So you're good at riding things."

Finn actually laughed so hard he had to pull the truck to a stop. "Really?" he asked as he looked at Rhys. "That's the best come-on a guy like you can come up with?"

It *had* been pretty lame and Rhys found himself smiling. "Guess so," he said good-naturedly and then relaxed. At least he had the proof he needed that he and Finn shared at least one important detail in common.

Finn got the truck moving again. "You must be from the city," the young man said as he looked Rhys up and down. God, it felt like a fucking caress.

"That obvious?"

Finn just smiled. "I'm guessing New York? Military? Cop?"

"Chicago and yes to both. Did two tours in Iraq, then joined the police academy. How'd you know?"

Shrugging, Finn replied, "You have that look in your eyes. The one men get when they've seen too much, too soon. You're what, late twenties?"

Rhys nodded.

"Eyes of an old man, body of a young one and you flirt worse than Ronny Elks, the first boy I kissed when I was fourteen. A damn shame," Finn said with a smile.

"How'd it work out for you and Ronny?"

"He married the captain of the cheerleading squad after he knocked her up junior year. He's so deep in the closet, I doubt he'll ever find his way out."

Rhys fingered the cowboy hat between them. It was the first time he could remember where the conversation with another man was actually that – conversation.

"Was it a good kiss at least?"

Finn glanced at him with a shy smile and nodded.

"So I guess there's hope for me yet," Rhys said.

"Guess so," Finn said with a grin. "We're here."

Rhys got out of the truck and looked around. Finn had parked in front of the barn rather than further up the hill where an old farmhouse sat. The small barn was weathered with faded red paint. To the left were a couple of small cottages that weren't in much better shape than the rest of the place. Behind the barn was a large, round paddock and beyond that was a sizeable pasture where a couple of horses were peacefully grazing on the little bits of green grass that sprouted up among the dry brush. Rhys knew absolutely nothing about ranching, horses, or cows, but even he could tell this place was barely hanging on.

"I know it doesn't look like much, but Cal's slowly bringing it back," Finn said defensively.

"Cal?"

"Callan Bale."

Rhys remembered the initials above the ranch sign he'd passed under just a few short minutes ago. "Right, the owner."

"Owner's son. Carter Bale owns the place. Cal's the foreman," Finn said. "Come on, I'll introduce you."

They passed through the open door of the barn and Rhys was instantly assaulted by the smell of hay and manure. All the stalls were empty.

"I thought this was a cow ranch."

"Don't let Cal hear you call them cows. Cattle," Finn said with a smirk. Rhys followed Finn out the back door of the barn to a small, circular arena where a dark brown horse stood in the center, a saddle cinched to its back. A man was doing something on the other side of the animal and Rhys could hear him murmuring to the horse in a soothing tone. He had no idea what the words were, but the husky tone was doing something to his insides.

"He's breaking him," Finn said, motioning to the man and horse.

Rhys must have looked confused because Finn smiled patiently. "Teaching him to accept the tack – the bridle and saddle – so he can be ridden. Cal found Astro at an auction last month. The previous owner couldn't handle him – hadn't even bothered to try and break him when he was younger. Just stuck him in a stall and ignored him."

They watched as Callan came around the horse, his big hands stroking over the animal's body. Rhys hadn't gotten a good look at the front of the other man, but the back was proving to be an impressive view. The man was tall, at least 6'2 and had a heavy build. Even with the chambray work shirt, Rhys could see wide shoulders, trim waist, perfect ass encased in faded denim, and thick thighs. Black hair stuck out from beneath the brown cowboy hat.

Callan continued talking to the horse as he began to loosen the saddle. A few seconds later, he was holding the heavy looking piece of tack in one hand, the horse's lead in the other. He turned and began walking towards them.

Rhys felt his body clench with need as gray-blue eyes met his. The man moved with easy, confident strength and when he reached the fence, he lifted the saddle onto it as if it weighed nothing. Thick, long fingers settled on the horse's neck as he turned his attention on Finn.

"You get the wire?"

"Yeah, it's in the truck." Finn shifted slightly.

He was hiding something, but apparently his boss recognized the look because Callan said, "What?"

Finn seemed to have trouble meeting Callan's gaze. Finally, he admitted, "I had to go to Hamilton to get it."

"Son of a bitch!" Callan snarled as he turned and led the horse out of the arena.

"Hamilton?" Rhys asked.

"Next town over – about thirty miles away," Finn said quietly.

Rhys knew there was more to the story, but decided to keep his mouth shut. Wasn't any of his business anyway. He just needed to keep his nose clean for the next six months and the best way to do that was keep his thoughts to himself.

Callan stalked past them, the horse in tow. He stopped just outside the barn and tied the horse to a post and snatched up the hose nearby and started washing the animal.

"I told you this would happen, Cal," Finn started.

"Don't, Finn. Just don't!" Callan replied angrily.

"I was talking to one of the ranch hands from that new place over in Corvallis. He says they're looking for hands and since none of them know about me…" Finn began.

Callan dropped the hose and strode over to Finn and grabbed him by the arm. "This is your home and those small-minded, homophobic, piece of shit cowards from town are not going to drive you from it. You hear me?" Callan nearly shouted. Rhys didn't miss the desire that flashed in Finn's eyes at being in such close proximity to the bigger man. So, the guy had a thing for his boss. Finn just nodded and Callan released him and returned to washing down the horse.

"Cal, this is Rhys Tellar," Finn finally said, as if just remembering Rhys' presence.

"You're Frank's friend, right?" Callan asked.

Rhys was still trying to piece together the information he'd just gleaned from Finn and Callan's conversation. Did Finn actually have to drive to another town to buy supplies because the people in the town of Dare refused to sell to a gay man? What the hell kind of back-woods place had Frank sent him to?

"Yeah," Rhys managed to say when Callan finally looked at him, his annoyance at Rhys' delay in answering clear.

"You ever worked around cattle before?"

"No," Rhys responded.

"Horses?"

"Nope," Rhys said as he steeled himself for the rejection that was about to come.

Callan untied the horse and began leading him into the barn. "Finn, show him around and get him started on the stalls, then come give me a hand with the fence."

CHAPTER 2

*R*hys felt every muscle burning as he shoveled the last pile of shit into the wheelbarrow and took it out to the mountain of steaming, smelly manure behind the barn. Being a cop had meant he had to keep in shape and working out had been the only thing to keep him from going insane in his tiny jail cell, so he'd figured a little physical labor wouldn't kill him. But between the searing heat and the backbreaking work, he was ready to throw in the towel and call Frank and beg the man to find him something else.

Finn had left a couple of hours ago after giving him a quick tour of the place and a run down on cleaning stalls and moving hay bales from the trailer out back. The only thing keeping him going was knowing tonight he'd be sharing one of the two small cottages with the very hot, very fuckable, Finn. That lean, toned body would fit perfectly beneath his as he stroked in and out of him with long, slow…

"You done?"

Finn's voice ripped him from his thoughts. "What?" he asked stupidly as he tried to get his growing erection under control before he had to turn and face the other man.

"I asked if you were done?"

"Um, yeah, just gotta line the last stall," he said as he pretended to try and get the last of the shit out of the already empty wheelbarrow.

"I'll take care of it," he heard Finn say.

By the time Rhys got back into the barn, Finn was putting fresh straw in the stall. Rhys put the wheelbarrow away, then stood in the entryway to the stall and watched the other man work. He was slightly shorter than Rhys' own 6 feet and was built like a swimmer with long, clean lines. His skin was golden from working in the hot Montana sun all day.

"So what was all that about earlier today? Hamilton?" Rhys asked. Finn glanced up, his blue eyes going dark and Rhys instantly regretted the question.

"Dare's not quite as forward thinking as Chicago probably is," Finn said quietly.

"Every place has haters," Rhys responded.

"Yeah, I suppose. But in a small town like Dare where there's one feed store, one grocery store, one hardware store, one gas station…" Finn's voice trailed off.

"You can't be the only gay guy in this place," Rhys said.

Finn finished what he was doing and went to walk past Rhys. Rhys extended his arm, forcing Finn to stop.

"What happened?" Rhys asked softly.

Finn sighed and leaned back against the doorframe, his shoulder brushing Rhys' hand. Electricity fired through Rhys' veins at the slight contact.

"Got caught making out with the mayor's son at our high school graduation party a while back. He told everyone I was trying to assault him. His father even tried to have me arrested." Finn leaned his head back against the wood and closed his eyes. "Cal has a friend who works for the State Patrol and he was able to smooth things over with the local cops, but the town still considers me a pervert. They've been punishing Cal ever since. The feed store was the last place I could still pick up supplies for the ranch, but that's gone now too."

"Jesus," Rhys muttered.

"I know I should take that job," Finn said as he opened his eyes

9

and fixed his gaze on Rhys. God, he really was beautiful and lust slammed through Rhys at the sight of those soft lips parting slightly as Finn spoke. Rhys couldn't stop himself from shifting so that his body lined up with Finn's, one arm still preventing Finn from escaping. He heard Finn suck in some air as Rhys let his erection brush up against Finn before putting just the tiniest amount of space between them.

"But you don't want to leave Callan," Rhys whispered as he skimmed his free hand over Finn's mouth. His lips felt like silk beneath his fingers and he really wanted to taste them. "You're in love with him."

Finn stiffened at Rhys' observation and tried to escape, but Rhys easily subdued him by pinning him with his body. The man instantly stopped struggling when he felt Rhys' dick pressed up against his own. It bothered Rhys that he was lusting after a guy who wanted someone else, but it wasn't like he was looking for wedding bells or even something beyond a couple of good, hard fucks. "Aren't you?" Rhys asked, wanting to hear the kid admit it.

"He's straight," Finn finally said.

Ouch. Poor kid. Out in a town filled with people that hated him for who he was and in love with a straight man on top of that. He was beginning to agree that Finn should cut his losses and get out of this place.

"But you're still in love with him." Rhys dragged his thumb back and forth over Finn's lower lip, then let out a harsh breath when Finn suddenly bit down gently on his finger and held it there as he stroked his tongue over the tip.

Rhys rubbed his cock against Finn's stiffening length for several long seconds and then nearly came when Finn pulled his finger into his mouth and sucked hard.

"Fuck," Rhys whispered as he dragged his finger free, fully prepared to replace it with his lips.

"Finn!"

Rhys pulled away from Finn who went pale at the sound of Callan's voice. They both turned to see the angry man standing just inside the doorway to the barn, his furious gaze pinning Finn. "Get the horses in."

Finn flushed and quickly disappeared from the stall and hurried out the back door.

"Mr. Tellar, come with me."

Rhys bristled at the order, but followed the man outside. They stopped near the pickup truck Finn had been driving earlier.

"Frank Pettit is a friend of mine, so when he asked me for a favor, I had no problem saying yes because I trust his judgement implicitly. But I won't hesitate to send your ass back to Chicago if you lay even one hand on Finn!"

So the guy could have given him a dozen different ultimatums for what would cause him to lose this job and he chose Finn? Interesting. Maybe he was more interested in the younger man then he let on.

"Sounds like Finn doesn't have a lot of options in this town," Rhys said casually.

"He doesn't have any *good* options, Mr. Tellar. And I definitely don't consider an ex-con who beat a cop half to death a good option for him."

Rhys bristled at that and fought the urge to take a swing at the other man. "You don't know shit about me," he managed to get out.

"And I don't need to. I told Frank I'd give you a chance. One chance. My guess is you won't even get through the week before you blow it," Callan said coldly.

"Fuck you."

Callan smirked as if Rhys' defensive words were more proof that he was right. "There's a room in the back of the barn. You'll be sleeping there instead of the staff quarters."

Callan started walking away. "You saw us, right, Mr. Bale?" When Callan stopped walking but didn't turn, Rhys said, "You saw what he was doing with his mouth?"

Rhys smiled in satisfaction when Callan stiffened. Maybe not as straight as Finn seemed to think. The thought was both disturbing and intriguing. "If he sucks dick the way he was sucking on my finger-"

Before he could finish his statement, Callan had him slammed back against the truck hard enough to rattle Rhys' teeth.

"Pack your shit and get the fuck out!"

"He's an adult-"

"He's nineteen, you asshole!"

That stopped Rhys short. "He said he worked here for six years."

"His father was the foreman here. Finn started helping out before and after school when he was thirteen years old!" Callan bellowed.

Rhys used his strength to push back against Callan, a move the other man clearly hadn't expected because they both froze when Rhys' erection brushed against the tell-tale hardness behind Callan's jeans. Rhys could have dismissed the hard-on if it wasn't for the raw need he saw in the other man's eyes. And in an instant the same lust that had him burning for Finn was back and focused on this man.

"Cal, let him go." Callan released him instantly at the sound of Finn's voice and put several feet of space between them and Rhys wondered how much Finn had heard. He watched in shock as Callan removed his cowboy hat and casually held it in front of the bulge in his pants.

Finn reached them and didn't seem to notice the sexual tension in the air or what Callan was doing with the hat. "You can't keep doing this Cal," Finn said sadly.

"Doing what?"

"Protecting me from everything. I'm not a kid anymore, despite what you think. Stop treating me like one."

"Finn-"

"He goes, I go," Finn said firmly, his eyes glancing in Rhys' direction.

Callan glanced over his shoulder and Rhys could feel the disdain in his bones. "He'll use you," Callan bit out.

"That's my choice to make."

The way they were talking like he wasn't even there left Rhys feeling cold and he moved past them both and headed towards Finn's little house. He hadn't even bothered to unpack before Finn put him to work so it took only a minute to grab his duffle bag from the closet in the small bedroom across from Finn's.

"I'm sorry, I didn't mean it to sound like I agreed that you would use me," Finn said from behind him.

"Doesn't matter. It's what I was planning to do," Rhys said as he slung the bag over his shoulder and turned to face Finn who was standing just inside the doorway.

"You don't have to go. Cal said you could stay," Finn offered.

"I don't think this is the best place for me to be right now," Rhys said as he tried to move past Finn. But the younger man refused to move out of his way.

"You thought I was older, didn't you?" Finn said. "He told you I'm nineteen."

"What else did you hear?"

"Just some yelling. When I came out, I saw he had you up against the truck." So the kid hadn't heard Rhys taunting Callan.

"Look kid," Rhys began, but stopped when Finn's face fell.

"I haven't been a kid since the day my dad beat the shit out of me when he found out I was gay!" Finn yelled angrily. "You know what? Fuck you! Fuck Cal!" he shouted before he disappeared into his room, slamming the door behind him. But before Rhys could even process what was happening, Finn ripped the door open, stalked across the hall and grabbed Rhys by the neck and slammed their mouths together.

Finn's tongue pressed into his mouth and he opened instantly and moaned as that slick, hot appendage stroked and twined around his own tongue. Finn's long fingers curled into his hair and angled Rhys' head the way he wanted it so he could go deeper and Rhys dropped his duffle bag and reached for Finn's hips. But Finn had other plans and quickly released him and stepped back. "Fuck you, Rhys," he whispered, his voice sad and heavy. The finality in his tone made something deep inside of Rhys twist, but before he could say anything, Finn went back to his room and closed the door, the sound of the lock engaging deafening to his ears.

CHAPTER 3

*J*esus, he never should have kissed the guy. Finn Stewart cursed his own stupidity for the hundredth time since he'd closed the door to his bedroom last night, securing the lock more to remind himself that he needed to stay in the room rather than as a signal to keep Rhys out. Between Cal and Rhys, he was riding high on unrequited desire and if Rhys had shown any interest beyond the kiss Finn had forced on him last night, Finn would have gotten into any position Rhys had told him to. Of course, it wouldn't have taken long for Rhys to figure out that he had no experience beyond kissing so things probably would have ended the way they had anyway – with Finn jerking off in the shower last night and Rhys on his way back to Chicago.

He glanced at the clock and saw his alarm would go off in less than five minutes. For once, he wasn't eager to face the day or the man he'd been pining over since he was old enough to figure out what lust actually was. He'd met Callan Bale when Cal's father hired Finn's own father as foreman. Finn's mom had walked out on them when he was seven and he hadn't heard from her since, but he and his dad had been close and he'd idolized the man. Tag Stewart had always made time for his son, even after long days running cattle and mending fences.

And as soon as Finn was old enough to sit a horse, he'd been learning the business by his father's side. They'd talked and planned endlessly about the day they would get their own ranch and run it together, side by side. And then a kiss with the mayor's son had taken it all away.

Growing up, he'd also gotten to work with Cal who was learning the business from his own father, Carter Bale, who'd inherited the ranch from Cal's grandfather. It hadn't taken long for Finn to realize that the feelings he had for Cal went well beyond being buddies or the way Cal often treated him like a younger brother. But Cal had never shown any interest in him and when Finn had finally gotten up the courage to try and kiss Cal after Finn's sixteenth birthday party, it had been a rude awakening.

He could still remember that night. The few friends he'd had over had gone home and his father had gone to bed and he and Cal had been sitting on the patio swing on Cal's porch. It had been just the two of them under a blanket of bright stars and the symphony of crickets and the occasional bullfrog from the nearby lake. Cal had given him a pocketknife and was in the process of explaining the different tools when Finn tried to kiss him. Cal had stopped him before their lips had touched and then looked at him with a sad smile – the one people gave you when they were trying to figure out how to let you down easy.

It turned out that Finn had been reading all the signals coming from Cal wrong over the years – the brush of his hand on Finn's shoulder had been meant as encouragement, the kind words meant to comfort. Somehow Finn had turned everything around in his young mind and it hadn't occurred to him that the strong feelings that went through him every time he was around Cal were one-sided. Cal hadn't even had to say anything after he prevented the kiss from happening – one pitying look was all it had taken to send Finn running and they'd never discussed it again.

After that, Finn had focused on saving enough money so that he could pitch in when it came time for him and his father to buy their own place. But then the mayor's son, Hunter Greene, had cornered him in his family's pool house during the senior graduation party and kissed him – his second ever since the brief, experimental kiss he'd shared with Ronny when they were both fourteen. Kissing Hunter had been like nothing he'd ever experienced before and it hadn't taken long before he and Hunter were rolling around on the floor, each trying to get their hands in the other's swimsuits. Finn had won the battle and had been on top of Hunter, stroking him with long, hard pulls as he humped against him. And then light had flooded the dark room and Hunter's father stood there as Hunter pushed Finn off and began spouting lies about what had transpired.

Before he could even explain what had really happened, Finn was being carted off to the police station and three hours later Cal was there to take him home. But home hadn't been the refuge it should have been and his father wasn't there to greet him with understanding. No, the man he'd loved more than anything, his hero, punched him over and over while calling him a faggot, then kicked him until Finn finally blacked out from the pain. He'd woken up in a hospital bed, Cal sitting worriedly in a nearby chair. He'd had that same bad news look on his face when he told Finn his father had left town after Cal fired him. Finn hadn't seen or heard from his father since.

Finn forced himself out of bed and went to the bathroom. His morning erection wouldn't be ignored so he climbed into the shower and took care of it, trying hard not to think too much about why his usual image of Cal taking him from behind suddenly included Rhys on his knees in front of him. By the time he'd toweled off, his need was already starting to burn through him again.

He got dressed and headed towards the kitchen and stopped suddenly at the sight that greeted him. Rhys was standing in front of the stove, his jeans lovingly hugging his tight ass and a grey T-shirt clinging to every rippling muscle along his back.

"Hey," Rhys said as he turned around, frying pan in one hand, spatula in the other. He began putting scrambled eggs on the two plates on the small kitchen table. God, the man was gorgeous and the heat from the kiss Finn had stolen last night came back with a vengeance, as did the hard-on he'd rubbed out just a few minutes ago.

Finn shifted to ease the tightness in his pants and heard Rhys ask, "You okay?" as his green eyes shimmered with amusement. *Bastard.*

"Fine," Finn managed to get out as Rhys turned back to the stove and put the pan down. The small microwave on the counter dinged and Rhys grabbed the bacon he'd been heating up.

"I made coffee," he said as he motioned to the nearly full pot.

"I thought you were leaving," Finn said irritably as he hunted for a mug, then filled it full with coffee.

"Changed my mind," was all Rhys said. He dropped bacon on both plates and began eating. Finn sat across from him, but didn't touch the food.

"Because I kissed you last night?" Finn finally asked. Rhys lifted his eyes. "Because that was a mistake," he stammered.

Rhys sighed and finished chewing before he responded, "I changed my mind because I don't want to go back to prison," he muttered.

Finn barely managed not to spit out the coffee he'd just taken a sip of. "Prison?"

"That's why I'm here. My parole officer knows Callan and pulled some strings to get me this job. Six months and I'll be free and clear. Otherwise I have to serve the rest of my sentence – two years."

"You said you were a cop," Finn said. It hadn't even occurred to Finn why someone like Rhys would be working at a ranch in Montana – he'd just assumed the guy needed a change of scenery or something.

"I *was* a cop," Rhys said bitterly, his tone making it clear he wasn't interested in discussing the subject further.

Finn decided to let it go and shoveled some food in his mouth. "It's good," he said as he reached for a piece of bacon.

"Yeah, well, when it's my turn to cook, it'll be this or spaghetti and that's it."

Finn chuckled. "I can live with that."

"And Finn," Rhys said, waiting until Finn raised his gaze and their eyes met. "Even if that kiss last night was a mistake, it was a fucking great one."

~

*F*inn watched Rhys shift awkwardly in the saddle as he tried to adjust to the horse's stride. "You good?" he asked as he pulled his own gelding up next to the mare Rhys was riding.

"Great," Rhys bit out.

"You look uncomfortable," Finn said.

"If you must know, my ass hurts like hell. And not in the good way!" Rhys snapped and Finn quickly had to adjust his seat at the image Rhys' statement had conjured up.

"It's only been twenty minutes," Finn said with amusement.

"Which is about nineteen minutes too long. Where the hell are the cows?" Rhys muttered as he fiddled with the reins.

"Probably over this hill. There's a river they like to hang out at in the afternoons."

Rhys mumbled something under his breath and Finn laughed. The man moved with easy confidence on the ground, but stick him on a horse and he was a mess. A hot mess though.

"You got anyone back in Chicago?" Finn asked, hoping a little conversation would relax Rhys enough so that riding would come a bit easier to him.

"You probably should have asked me about a boyfriend last night before you kissed the shit out of me."

Finn felt the heat in his cheeks at the reminder of his brazen behavior as well as the fact that it turned out that Rhys had enjoyed it. "I meant family."

"No. No family. No boyfriend either," Rhys smirked.

"Where are your folks?"

"No idea. Grew up in foster care. Never found out who my real parents were."

"Sorry," Finn said.

"For what?" Rhys said casually – too casually.

"So no one you were close to?"

"Not really. One of my foster brothers and I joined the army at the same time, but he stayed in after I finished my last tour and we lost touch. What about you?"

Finn stiffened. He hadn't meant for the conversation to swing towards him. But fair was fair. He couldn't very well expect Rhys to open up if he wasn't willing to do the same. "My mom left when I was seven. I never knew why – one day she was there, one day she wasn't. And I already told you about my dad."

"You said he beat the shit out of you. What happened?" Rhys asked softly.

Finn quickly told him about what had happened between him and Hunter.

"So your dad didn't know you were gay before that?"

Finn shook his head. "It honestly never occurred to me to tell him. We were so close that I figured he wouldn't care. I guess reading people has never been my strong suit," Finn said with a self-deprecating laugh.

"You read me pretty well," Rhys said. Before Finn could respond, Rhys asked, "What happened after your dad heard about you and the mayor's son?"

"After Cal fixed everything with the cops, he took me home. My dad and I lived in the foreman's house – that little one next to ours – and Cal dropped me off and said he'd check back in with me after my dad and I had a chance to talk. I didn't even get to tell my Dad my side of the story – he just started hitting me the second I walked in the door. Kept calling me a faggot. I guess Cal must have waited outside or something because he was the one who pulled him off of me. I'm not sure what happened after that. Cal doesn't really talk about it. I woke up in the hospital and Cal told me Dad was gone. I heard he got a job at a ranch in Wyoming, but not really sure."

They rode in silence for a while before Rhys said, "You can ask me, you know."

"Ask you what?" Finn said even though he knew.

Rhys snorted and said. "I went to prison for assaulting another cop. My partner."

"What did he do?"

Rhys shot him a sharp look. "What makes you think *he* did something?"

"Dunno – guess you don't strike me as the type to go after someone unless you were provoked." Rhys was silent for a long time, studying him until Finn felt the need to squirm in his saddle.

"He used our personal relationship to sell information on one of my CIs," Rhys finally said.

"CI?"

"Confidential Informant. I worked Narcotics and busted a kid for possession. Turned out that he'd gotten mixed up with a gang and witnessed the murder of a rival dealer so I worked with the DA to get the kid a deal. The dealer he'd been working for was someone the Feds had been trying to put away for years so they agreed to put him in protective custody until the trial, then Witness Protection."

"What happened?" Finn asked when Rhys fell silent, seeming to get lost in the past.

"My partner on the force was also my lover. I trusted him one hundred percent so when he came to my place I never even thought to put away the information I had on my CI. Turned out my partner had been working for the dealer for years and he sold the kid's location to him. The kid, his mother and his protective detail were murdered the day before the trial. The dealer walked away scot free."

"Fuck," Finn whispered.

"I was one of only a few people who knew where the kid had been stashed so I knew the leak could have come from me. Tom was the only person in my life that could have been involved so I confronted him. He admitted it. Said no one would believe a rookie cop's word over someone who'd been on the force for fifteen years. I just wish I'd killed the fucker before they pulled me off of him." The venom in Rhys' voice was chilling.

Finn moved his horse closer to Rhys' so their legs brushed together and that seemed to pull the other man out of the dark place he'd gone. "What happened to him?" Finn asked.

"He spent three weeks in coma. Woke up just in time to watch me get sentenced to four years in prison. He was right – I had no proof and he had a stellar reputation. I ended up taking a plea deal that made it possible to get a sentence that gave me chance at parole. Said all the right things at my parole hearing."

"How long were you in there for?"

"Two years. Spent most of it in solitary since being a cop in prison doesn't make you a lot of friends," Rhys said with a bitter laugh.

Finn shuddered at what Rhys was saying. He reached down and grabbed the mare's reins and pulled her to a stop, then put his hand over one of Rhys'.

"I'm sorry, Rhys. I'm sorry that happened to you."

CHAPTER 4

*R*hys wished to God that he wasn't sitting on a horse at the moment because he wanted nothing more than to lean over and kiss the beautiful mouth that was offering words of comfort, not judgement. Finn had surprised him when he'd automatically assumed that Rhys had been provoked into assaulting someone else. And now he saw no condemnation in those gentle eyes. Finn absolutely believed everything Rhys had told him and he was surprised at the relief that went through him. It shouldn't have been important. No one else had believed him, not even his own attorney. Even Frank seemed doubtful about his story so to have this young man who didn't know him from Adam believe him was humbling.

Emotion welled up inside so Rhys only managed a nod before Finn pulled back and they continued the ride in silence. Finn's kiss the night before had messed with his head as well as his body. He'd made it to the front door last night, but couldn't bring himself to walk out. He didn't want to be on the ranch and Callan definitely didn't want him there, but that kiss had changed everything. Sure, it had been done out of anger after Rhys' had poked at Finn's age by calling him a kid, but the impact of those lips on his had done him in both physically and emotionally. He wanted Finn. Badly. And not just physically

– he found himself craving Finn's smile, hearing that ridiculously enthusiastic laugh. He wanted those soft looks and warm touches that he'd never quite managed to share with any of his other lovers. He wanted Finn to want him the way Finn wanted Callan.

God, how had things gotten this fucked up, this fast? How could one kiss have had him turning back around from that front door and crawling into that empty bed, wishing he were anything but alone? At least before Finn had kissed him, he'd had the hope of being able to pass the time in this hell hole by being fuck buddies with his new roommate. But his gut was telling him that Finn wasn't the type for a no-strings attached relationship and Rhys definitely wasn't looking for more than a hook-up. So where did that leave him? The friend zone? With a guy he was undeniably attracted to? Did he really want to spend the next six months watching the guy he was lusting after make moon eyes at Callan? And he couldn't even think about the moment of lust he'd felt towards the dark-haired man that had towered over him when he had him pressed up against that truck.

Rhys' attention returned to the present when Finn said, "Look. Down there."

They'd reached the top of the small hill and below them was a thin strip of water that dozens of black cows were standing around, some picking at the brown grass, others wading into the dirty water. "Is that all of them?"

Finn sighed. "Yeah, that's all of them," he said quietly as he urged his horse down the hill towards the herd. Rhys could tell there was plenty he wasn't saying.

"Something happened," Rhys said. A statement, not a question.

Finn cast him a glance. "Couple years ago we had nearly 300 head. Not as big as most places around here, but Cal had mixed some good breeding stock and was getting well above market price."

"And?" Rhys prodded.

"And then Cal decided not to fire the queer like everyone told him to. Suddenly the cost of everything went up but prices fell. Fences got cut in the middle of the night. Nearly half the herd died when the main water supply was poisoned."

"Jesus."

"Cops couldn't find any suspects of course so they said it was probably an industrial accident or something upstream. Funny how only our stock was affected. Cal had to sell off most of the remaining herd to stay in the black. He says we're back on track…"

"But you don't believe him."

"I'm gonna take a quick circle around the herd to make sure everyone looks okay. You mind checking out the fence over there for breaks?" Finn asked, effectively ending the conversation. He didn't even give Rhys a chance to answer before he was urging his horse off to check the herd. Rhys managed to do his part and inspect the fence, though steering the horse was proving to be a continuous struggle and he finally dismounted and walked the horse as he checked for any damage. The ride back to the barn was quiet and Finn seemed uncharacteristically withdrawn.

"You okay?" Rhys asked as they began brushing down the horses.

Finn just nodded, then asked, "You mind washing West down for me?" as he motioned to his horse.

"No problem," Rhys said and watched Finn disappear out of the barn.

Rhys grabbed his horse's lead as well as the big grey horse's and led both animals to the wash area he'd seen Callan use yesterday. Neither animal gave him a hard time as he ran lukewarm water over them which he was grateful for since he had no clue what the hell he was doing.

It wasn't until he started on the grey horse that he finally noticed Callan leaning in the doorway of the barn, his intense eyes focused on him. Waiting for him to fuck up, he imagined. Rhys felt a shiver go through him as he felt the gaze burning into him and his jeans instantly felt tight.

"You need to use release knots." He turned to see that Callan had closed the distance between them and was loosening one of the nylon lead ropes that he'd tied in a knot around the post. "You really don't know shit, do you?" Callan muttered.

Rhys forced himself to keep his mouth shut, reminding himself that any crap this guy spewed at him would still be better than two more years in a windowless jail cell.

"Where's Finn?" Callan asked as he finally worked the first lead free.

"He needed some space."

Callan scowled. "What did you do to him?"

Rhys shook his head and let out a humorless laugh. "Jesus, you really do treat him like a fucking kid."

"I look out for him," Callan snapped.

"Yeah? And how's that working out for you? For him?" Rhys quipped.

Rhys was surprised when Callan didn't respond and even more so when he actually saw a flash of pain in the other man's eyes. "Hey man," Rhys started, but Callan cut him off.

"You need to use a release knot when you secure a horse so in case something spooks them, you can get them free quickly so they don't hurt themselves." Callan looped the lead around the post and demonstrated. Once it was secured, he pulled one end quickly and the whole lead unfurled. "A leg injury on a horse can be a death sentence," Callan said softly as one of his big hands fondly stroked the grey horse's face. Finn's horse. Rhys felt water drip onto his leg and realized he'd been staring at those fingers curling around the animal's muzzle.

"You try," Callan said as he handed Rhys the lead and took the hose from him. Their fingers brushed and Rhys felt it everywhere. Callan must have felt something too because he stilled, his gaze holding Rhys' without mercy. Rhys forced himself to be the one who moved first and his fingers felt awkward and heavy as he tried to mimic the knot. He held his breath as Callan's hands closed over his and guided him through the moves.

Jesus, what the fuck was happening to him? His stomach was rolling with nerves and he actually found himself leaning in towards Callan before he realized what he was doing. Jerking back, Rhys quickly undid the tie for the horse he'd been riding and reworked it. Somehow he got it tied correctly and was both pleased and disappointed. As much as he'd like having Callan's hands on him, he needed to end this before he did something stupid. Not only was the guy playing it straight for some reason, the man clearly hated him, not to mention that Finn, someone he was already considering a friend, had been hung up on this man for a while.

"Good," Callan murmured as he checked the second tie, then stepped back. "I spoke with Frank last night to let him know you made it okay."

Callan's words were like ice water being dumped on his emotions. This man thought of him as a loser. Had said as much yesterday when he'd been warning Rhys off Finn. "Yeah?" he said coolly as he took the hose back from Callan and focused all his attention on getting the horses cleaned up.

"He said to call him if you need anything."

"Right," Rhys said.

"Tell Finn I'll be up at the main house if he needs me," Callan said.

Rhys nodded and finally took his first deep breath once Callan had disappeared back into the barn. God, how the fuck was he ever going to make it six months around these two men?

CHAPTER 5

*C*allan Bale tamped down on his runaway lust as he left the barn and headed up the driveway towards the main house. His eyes automatically searched the area for Finn since it was unlike him to disappear while they were still working. It was even more unusual for him to abandon his horse to someone else's care. He'd given the gelding to Finn himself as a graduation present. It had been the same day that Finn's whole life had changed because he had the courage to be who he was and wouldn't be relegated to playing a role just to please those around him. As young and innocent as Finn was, he was still a hell of a lot braver than Callan would ever be.

Callan had known long before he met Finn Stewart that he preferred men to women. But unlike Finn, he'd tested the waters only when distance offered him the anonymity he needed. His first sexual experience with a man hadn't even happened until his sophomore year of college when he and his roommate had gotten more than a little drunk and Callan had gotten his first blowjob. But the morning after had been nearly comical as both he and his roommate played dumb and pretended nothing had happened. Two days later his roommate had transferred to a new dorm so he could supposedly be closer to his classes and Callan had found himself spending the rest of the semester dating one flighty coed after the other.

He'd been the ripe old age of twenty-one when he finally fucked another man for the first time. He'd spent the night of his birthday doing what all college guys were expected to do – bar hop with his buddies and his shiny new ID to prove he was legal. But the next night he'd snuck out on his own and went to a gay club on the outside of town he'd passed more than once on his way home each weekend to help his father at the ranch. The club had offered every kind of guy imaginable, but it had been a tattooed, muscle head named Mav that had dragged him into one of the bathroom stalls and kissed the shit out of him. Any hope that he'd be able to find the same level of sexual gratification with a woman ended the second he buried his cock deep inside the other man's ass as he bent him over the toilet.

He'd gone back the next night and found another guy who'd blown him in the alley behind the club. And that had been how he'd spent most nights during his last year of school. Going to class and flirting with pretty girls during the day, fucking random men on the nights he could no longer deny the craving. And then one night he'd met the wrong man and he'd ended up broken and bleeding in an alley next to a dumpster. The trip to the ER had been a lesson in humiliation and when the cops had made it clear that anyone and everyone would find out the circumstances of what had been done to him, Callan took them up on their offer to 'forget the whole thing' and had scurried back to his dorm room with instructions to get tested for the whole gamut of STDs for the next six months. And when his father had asked him the next time he went home why he was limping and where the bruises on his face had come from, the lie that he'd been mugged had fallen easily from his lips.

There'd been no men since that night and anytime he had the urge, all it took was the memory of being brutalized to deflate his dick faster than air seeping out of a flat tire. Until Finn. Callan smiled to himself as he remembered the sight of the gangly, pimply faced boy that had been introduced to him when Callan was twenty-five and working for his father full-time. From that day forward, thirteen-year-old Finn had stuck to him like glue and never stopped talking for longer than a minute or two.

Callan hadn't had a brother or sister so it had been strange to adjust to the ever-present kid tagging along and trying to mimic everything he did, but at some point things changed and he actually missed Finn when he was at school. But he noticed a change in Finn after he turned fifteen. The kid's hero worship had turned into something else, something deeper and Callan had tried to pull back since he knew where Finn's infatuation would ultimately lead. He was certain that after Finn's disastrous sixteenth birthday that he would lose the only friend he really had, but Finn had always been the better man, even before he was actually a man, and he'd let Callan ease them back to what they'd been before the almost-kiss.

Keeping the truth about his own sexuality from Finn had been difficult, especially in the times he could tell that Finn needed someone to talk to about what he was going through after the ruinous episode with the mayor's son and his father's brutal assault, but Callan had been a coward because being honest about who and what he was would mean he'd lose everything he'd worked for. But as Finn had grown and matured, Callan's body began to betray him and he found it harder to deny that he craved Finn in a way that wasn't okay for someone who may as well have been his little brother. Not to mention the twelve-year age difference between them.

And since his life wasn't already fucked up enough, God had apparently thought it amusing to send Rhys Tellar barreling into their lives. Not only was his own attraction to the other man palpable, seeing him with Finn had him burning with hate and lust at the same time. When he'd seen them nearly kiss in that stall yesterday, part of him had wanted to stop it but a darker part had wanted to join them – to order them both to their knees and let them taste each other while their tongues were wrapped around his cock.

"Callan honey, is that you?" he heard his Aunt Dolly's voice call out as he pushed open the screen door to the main house. Hearing her voice quelled any hard-on that had been forming at the image that had managed to imprint itself in his brain only seconds earlier.

"Yeah, it's me," he responded as he made his way to the kitchen.

Dolly was covered in flour so he pressed a kiss to her cheek and snagged one of the fresh cookies she had cooling on a baking rack on the counter. She was a petite woman and he marveled that she and his father had come from the same parents, considering their differences in size and coloring. Dolly didn't even hit the 5-foot mark in heels while his own father was closer to Callan's 6'2. Age had taken a harsh toll on his father, but Dolly, though she was three years older than her brother, still acted spry. She'd been in their lives for just the past few years as his father's health deteriorated, but with her loving and open nature it felt like she'd been there forever. He reached for another cookie, but she snatched the baking rack out of his reach and began putting the cookies in a plastic container.

"These are for Finn," she said. "And your new man."

A surge went through Callan at hearing Rhys described as his man even though he knew Dolly hadn't meant it that way.

"What's his name again?"

"Rhys."

"Yes. Invite them both to dinner tomorrow night," she commented as she reached into the oven to get the next batch of cookies out.

"Probably not a good idea," Callan said as he pulled a glass from the cupboard and filled it with water from the kitchen sink.

"How come? Finn hasn't stopped by for dinner in such a long time…"

Callan stiffened as he heard footsteps shuffling into the kitchen. "I don't want that little queer in my house," his father said.

"Carter!" Dolly said in shock.

Callan forced himself to take in a deep breath and put the glass carefully down on the counter, afraid that otherwise he'd end up shattering it. "I told you what I would do if you called him that again-" Callan began.

"Callan, don't," he heard Dolly say behind him, then felt her hand close around his arm. "He doesn't know what he's saying," she whispered.

Carter opened the refrigerator and searched through it, seemingly oblivious to the danger he faced from his own son. "Sarah, where's my beer?"

Dolly's fingers tensed on Callan's arm, then she brushed past him. "Carter, it's me, Dolly. Your sister. Sarah's gone, remember?"

His father looked at her with a mix of confusion and irritation, then repeated, "Where's my beer?"

"No beer. It mixes with your medication," she reminded him gently. "Why don't you go sit down in the den and watch some TV and I'll bring you something to eat?"

Carter harrumphed, then shuffled back the way he'd come.

"He didn't mean that, honey," Dolly said as she began pulling things out of the fridge. He wanted to tell her that his father's bigotry had been around long before the dementia, but she tended to cling to the fond memories of the baby brother she'd grown up with. Not that Callan could blame her since she needed something to hang on to since she was stuck with the temperamental man day in and day out while Callan tried to keep the ranch afloat. "How about tomorrow night I make some extra lasagna and you and your boys can have it down at your house?" she said brightly.

Another pang at hearing Finn and Rhys referred to as his hit him hard. He needed to get a grip. "Sure," he said, though he knew there was no way he could sit down for a meal with the both of them.

"You want me to make you a sandwich?" Dolly asked as she began putting ingredients together for the brother that would have forgotten about the sandwich and her by the time she brought it to him in the den.

"No, thanks. I gotta get back to work," he said.

"Here. Tell those boys I'll be down to see them real soon," she said with a smile as she handed him the container full of cookies. "And you stay out of those – you can come back and get yours later."

He forced a smile to his face and gave her a kiss on the cheek. She didn't deserve this life and he wished he could change things – find a way to come up with enough money to get his father the care he needed and finally set Dolly free. Muttering a quick thanks, he hurried out of the house and began the short walk back down to the small foreman's house he was using. After Callan had kicked Finn's father off the property, he and Finn had shared the small house until gradually the few ranch hands that he'd managed to keep had started to leave one by one. Once it was just him and Finn, it had made more sense to move Finn to the other house. He'd tried to tell himself it had nothing to do with the alarming level of desire he'd begun to feel for Finn. But like the rest of his life, it was a big, fat, fucking lie.

~

F inn stiffened when he heard the footsteps behind him, already knowing who the heavy tread belonged to.

"Thought I'd find you here," he heard Cal say.

An open, plastic container was shoved under Finn's nose and the smell of butterscotch assaulted him. He couldn't help but smile as he took the container and grabbed one of the still warm cookies. Dolly had to be sent from above, he thought to himself as he automatically handed the cookie to Cal and then grabbed one for himself.

"You okay?" Cal asked him.

It was one of Cal's favorite questions and Finn used to love hearing it because it was a reminder that no matter what, Cal was always looking out for him. Knowing that had always made Finn feel strong – even with all the battles he faced, Cal had his back. But now the words were just more dead weight on his shoulders. He used to feel like Cal's equal and that even though they would never have more than friendship between them, at least Finn could contribute, could help Cal realize his dream of running a successful ranch. Working together had become so easy and natural that he didn't really even think of Cal as his boss any more. They'd become partners, family even.

"Fine," Finn said automatically. "I miss it," he said, motioning to empty swath of dirt in front of them.

Cal sighed. "Me too. But filling it in was the only option. Even if we had built a fence around it to keep the herd out, the wildlife would have suffered. The DNR guy said there was no way to get the poison out of the water."

They were both silent for a long time, the early evening air warm and quiet around them. "You have to let me go, Cal," Finn said quietly.

He didn't have to look at Cal to see the stiff set in his jaw or the tension in his frame. Cal had been trying to protect him since Finn's father cast him out of his life – before then actually.

"No, I need you here," Cal said stubbornly.

Finn dropped his head onto his knees. "What's to stop them from coming after the horses next? Or Dolly? Or You?"

"I can take care of us. All of us."

Finn wished he could put his head on Cal's shoulder. Even if just for a moment so he could absorb some of that unfailing faith that everything would work out okay. But something had changed since he kissed Rhys last night, and he hadn't realized it until now. If he stayed with Cal, he'd never have a chance to try and build a life with someone else. Someone like Rhys. He knew Rhys wasn't sticking around either so pursuing something with the other man wasn't an option, but he'd enjoyed getting to know Rhys this afternoon. He'd liked that little flutter in his belly when Rhys had shamelessly flirted with him yesterday in the truck and he hadn't felt that full on rush of lust he'd had when Rhys had held him in place in the stall in a long time...not since he'd accepted the fact that Cal would never see him that way. Staying here was not only dragging Cal and the ranch down, it was slowly eating away at the hope Finn had for any kind of a future with another person.

"I'll get Rhys up to speed before I go," he heard himself saying as pain clenched his insides.

"No." That was it. One word. No argument, no discussion. It was too much. Finn shot to his feet, ignoring the cookies that spilled all over the ground.

"Did you ever think I might need something more than this, Cal? That I might need a life outside of Dare? To be some place where I don't have to be looking over my shoulder all the time? Where I don't need to listen to people call me names under their breath?" Cal refused to look at him and that had Finn kicking at the dirt in anger. "I can't even go in to your father's fucking house, Cal!"

He saw Cal clench his jaw hard and he instantly felt guilty because he knew Cal's loyalty to his family ran as deep as the obligation the man felt towards him. Some of the anger left him and he squatted down next to Cal and said, "What about marriage? Kids? You think I could ever have those things here? Do you think there will be a day where you and your wife and me and my husband can go out for dinner together in this town?"

Finn reached out to gently touch Cal's arm and he felt the muscles tighten beneath his palm. He drew his hand back and softly said, "I need to go someplace where all those things are okay. Where I don't have to fight every fucking day just to be who I am."

Finn felt tears stinging his eyes so he stood and stepped back. "I need you to want those things for me, Callan," he said firmly, then turned and left the clearing.

~

allan. Finn had called him Callan. He'd started calling him "Cal" shortly after they met and he was the only one who'd ever done it and now Finn was taking even that away from him. Callan flung the container of cookies across the pile of dirt that used to be the cold, clear lake he and Finn would swim in after a long day's work.

He had no doubt that Finn would carry through with his decision this time and it was absolutely the right thing for him to do. Finn deserved everything he'd ask Callan to want for him, but all Callan really wanted to do was track the man down and fuck him until he promised he'd never leave. He wanted to bury his body so deep inside of Finn's that a piece of him would always be there. But what Finn needed was the one thing Callan couldn't give. He couldn't choose Finn over his family…over the commitment he'd made to his mother to always take care of his father after she was gone.

His father may have been a cold-hearted bastard at times, but he'd taken care of Callan, had put him through school, taught him the business. And he'd loved Callan's mom deeply. Maybe if things had been different, if his father hadn't started to lose himself in the darkness of his own mind, Callan could have walked away – forced his father to accept him or let him go. But that choice had been taken away the same as the man's other memories. What kind of person would he be if he abandoned his own father? Left Aunt Dolly to care for him by herself? He knew the answer – the kind of person someone as good and kind as Finn could never love.

CHAPTER 6

*R*hys heard the front door open and waited expectantly for the sound of footsteps to make their way to the kitchen to join him. Several seconds passed and all he heard was the sound of another door closing. Rhys put the box of spaghetti noodles he'd been about to cook down and turned off both burners on the stove. He went to Finn's room and knocked softly on the closed door. There was no response so he tried the knob. Locked just like last night.

Finn had been a no-show since he disappeared after their ride and Rhys had been on edge ever since his run in with Callan. A smarter man would have gone back to the kitchen, made himself a shitload of spaghetti that he could inhale while watching whatever piece of crap movie was on the twenty-year-old TV in the living room and called it a night. But no one had ever really accused Rhys of being too smart so he pounded his fist on the door.

"Finn, open up!"

Nothing.

Rhys felt a shadow of panic skitter down his back at the continued silence. He'd known the young man for barely twenty-four hours, but Rhys knew quiet and withdrawn weren't Finn's thing, so he hurried into his own room and pulled out the small, black nylon pouch he kept stashed in his bag. He went back to Finn's door, found the tool he wanted and picked the lock.

"Finn?" Rhys said softly as he stepped into the room which was cast in shadows as the sun fell.

"I can't, Rhys. Not tonight," he heard Finn whisper and his eyes tracked the sound to the body curled up on the far side of the bed.

"Can't what?" Rhys asked gently as he went to the side of the bed Finn was laying on and knelt in front of him. Finn's eyes were closed and Rhys could see the dampness along his cheeks.

"Eat, drink, talk, fuck," he said pointedly. "Can't," he repeated, his voice hollow.

Rhys actually hurt for Finn and he found himself reaching out to stroke his face. "Okay."

Finn squeezed his eyes closed even harder at the contact and Rhys guessed the younger man was barely holding it together. He stood up, but instead of leaving, he went around the other side of the bed and worked his boots off.

He felt Finn stiffen when Rhys crawled into the bed next to him and pulled him back against his chest.

"Rhys-" Finn started to say as he tried to get free.

Rhys tightened his grip and dropped his mouth next to Finn's ear. "Just let me hold you, Finn. Nothing else," he said quietly and felt relief go through him as Finn relaxed against him. Any desire he might have felt at that moment was quashed when a shudder and harsh sob went through Finn and Rhys did the only thing he could think to do – he held him tighter.

～

*R*hys woke up alone in Finn's bed the next morning. He hadn't felt Finn leave the bed, but Rhys had been awake most of the night as Finn tossed and turned in his sleep. Of all the men Rhys had been with, only Tom had ever spent the night and the other man most definitely hadn't been a cuddler, so having someone pressed up against him all night long had been a new and surprisingly pleasant experience. They'd started off with Finn's back pressed to Rhys' front and the feel of Finn's firm ass nudging his cock every time the man moved had left Rhys both grateful and disappointed that he'd left his jeans on when he'd gotten into Finn's bed. By the time Finn had drifted off to sleep, then turned around and snuggled up against Rhys' chest, Rhys was in physical agony and had to reach between their mashed up bodies to loosen the button and fly on his jeans. He just hoped to God Finn hadn't noticed. And he really hoped the erection he was now sporting hadn't been there when Finn got up.

Rhys forced himself out of bed and went back to his room to get cleaned up. His eyes burned from the lack of sleep and his muscles protested every move as he stripped off his clothes and climbed into the shower. He hadn't even been at the job for two full days yet and he was feeling it everywhere. No wonder Callan and Finn had such hard bodies – every muscle had been earned.

A sudden image of Callan and Finn wrapped around him had Rhys reaching for his cock. Rhys was equal opportunity when it came to playing top or bottom, but now he was wondering if he could take both men at once. The idea of them filling him up at the same time, working in tandem as they stroked in and out of him had him desperately pulling at his dick. It would be Callan's heavy weight that held him down as Finn pumped up into him from below, his and Callan's dicks rippling and pulsing inside of Rhys. His own dick would be pressed between him and Finn and it would only take the slightest touch of Finn's firm grip to end him.

"Fuck!" Rhys shouted as his release shot through him without warning and he slapped the tile hard with his free hand to keep himself upright. The orgasm seemed endless as lines of seed coated the shower wall and mixed with the hot water. When the shuddering finally eased, he dropped his forehead against his arm and then let out a soft chuckle. Jesus, he was so fucked.

≈

*F*inn ran the brush gently over West's face as the animal pressed his large head against Finn's chest. The horse had been a perfect fit for him, though that shouldn't surprise him since Cal had been the one to gift him with the animal two years ago. Cal had always seemed to know what he needed so the fact that he'd been given a spirited, but nearly bomb-proof mount was just another indication of how Cal wanted, no, needed to protect him. It was scary to think of life beyond this ranch, beyond Cal.

It had taken everything in him last night not to go running back to Cal's side and tell him that he had changed his mind, that he would stay. So he'd forced himself to walk until that need had lessened and then made himself go back to the tiny house he was sharing with the other man who had unwittingly changed his life. It wasn't that he blamed Rhys for opening his eyes to what was missing, but it hadn't made facing the man any easier so he'd snuck off to his room to lick his wounds.

He hadn't been surprised when the locked door failed to keep the former cop out, but the feel of Rhys pulling him tight against his own body had opened something up inside of Finn that he feared he'd never be able to close off again. And the truly eye-opening part had been that what Rhys had done hadn't been about sex. Painting Rhys as a just a horny, one-night stand kind of guy had been the one thing that made it possible for Finn to keep him at arm's length and now even that was gone. Finn sighed and dropped his forehead against West's. He was in love with one man who would never want him back and now his body ached for another who would inevitably walk away from him.

"Morning," he heard Rhys say as he entered the barn and he felt the heat of the other man's body as he stopped behind him.

"Morning," Finn said back, not trusting himself to turn around. He couldn't let this man see any more of his weakness than he already had.

"You been up a while?"

Finn casually shrugged, then pulled back from West and unclipped the horse from the cross ties. Rhys didn't need to know that he'd woken well before the alarm was set to go off and had just lain there while he reveled in the feel of Rhys' arms wrapped around him or that he'd wondered what it would be like to wake Rhys with a deep, lingering kiss on those firm lips – the ones he'd only gotten a brief taste of two nights ago. Had it really only been two days since Rhys turned his world upside down?

"What's the plan for today?" Rhys asked as he glanced in each empty stall. "You already cleaned?" he said as Finn turned West around and started leading him out of the barn.

"Yeah. Cal's horse is gone so he probably already went to check on the herd. The water trough in the main pasture needs to be emptied and cleaned and then we need to start thinning the manure pile. Spreader's been broken for a couple months so we'll have to do it by hand," he called over his shoulder. He smiled at the colorful curse Rhys let out and then walked West to the pasture.

∼

*R*hys knew he'd die a happy man if he never had to shovel another pile of horseshit for the rest of his life. He'd tried to draw Finn into casual conversation throughout the morning, but the young man had remained stubbornly mute. Rhys still had no clue what had happened between their ride yesterday and Finn's break-down last night. It was like the good-natured guy he'd met two days ago had vanished and left a hollow shell of flesh and bone in his place. He reminded himself that his plan was to stay out of it, but as he watched Finn work himself to the point that he could barely stand, Rhys bit out a curse and grabbed Finn's arm.

"Let's take a break," he said as he dragged Finn over to the wash stall and turned on the hose.

"I'm fine," Finn insisted.

"Yeah, I know. So you've said," Rhys said dryly. He cleaned his hands and arms off, then lowered his head so he could run the hose over it. The water wasn't cold, but it still felt good as it slid down his hair and seeped into his shirt. He shoved the hose into Finn's hands and gave him a warning look. Several seconds passed before Finn finally cleaned his own arms and hands off, then used his hands to slick some water through his hair.

"You going to tell me what happened last night between you and Callan?" he finally asked.

Finn turned off the water and wrapped the hose up. For a long time, he thought maybe Finn wouldn't answer him, but then he finally said, "Gave him my notice."

"Good," Rhys said.

~

*F*inn was caught off guard by the response. "Good?" he echoed softly. He'd expected some big argument or demand for an explanation.

"Yeah. About fucking time," Rhys muttered as he went into the barn and started pulling down the individual water buckets from each stall.

The lack of sympathy irritated Finn. "Why do you say that?"

"Because you deserve better," Rhys said without hesitation or guile, instantly wiping out the building anger that had been growing inside of Finn. He'd been expecting Rhys to berate him for waiting things out as long as he had.

"Better than what?" Finn asked him.

Rhys looked up from what he was doing, his dark gaze pinning Finn's. "Just better," he answered before releasing the bucket from the clip holding it in place and stepping outside the stall, his body brushing Finn's slightly as he moved past him.

Finn didn't stop to think about the repercussions of what he was doing. Instead, he grabbed Rhys' free arm and stopped his forward motion. They stood like that for several long seconds before something passed through Rhys' dark eyes and then that mouth was crashing down on his. The water bucket hit the floor spraying water over both of them as Rhys wrapped his arms around Finn and dragged him up along his body as his tongue thrust into Finn's mouth.

Nothing had prepared Finn for the overwhelming sensations that crashed through him as Rhys claimed him. Even the kiss from a couple nights ago paled with what was happening to him now. Sparks fired beneath his skin as Rhys' fingers dug into his hips and that lush tongue explored every corner of Finn's mouth. Something knotted in his belly and his cock pushed against his jeans painfully. He needed more, though he wasn't completely sure what more meant.

Finn needed something to hang on to so he wrapped his arms around Rhys' back and curled his hands over the other man's shoulders. He felt one of Rhys' hands stroke his ass and then those amazing fingers were pushing under the waistband of his jeans, the rough skin searching out the small of his back, then gliding lower. Finn moaned at the feel of Rhys' fingers exploring his crease and he had to rip his mouth free of Rhys' so he could suck in a breath. Their cocks brushed as Rhys pulled him closer and fastened his lips on his neck and sucked hard. Marking him.

"Finn!"

Finn ripped free of Rhys at the sound of Cal's voice and looked around frantically. Cal was calling him from outside somewhere so he hadn't seen what they'd been doing. Relief flooded through him and he turned back to Rhys, but froze when he saw the anger simmering in the other man's eyes.

"Rhys," Finn started, knowing he'd just royally fucked up.

"Finn!" Cal shouted again.

"Don't worry about it," Rhys muttered as he wiped his hand over his lips as if trying to get rid of Finn's taste. Pain and disappointment went through Finn at the sight. He followed Rhys to the back door and saw Cal pulling his horse to a stop. A small, black calf was draped over his lap, blood dripping down its sides.

"Call Doc Sanders," he said to Finn. "Rhys, give me a hand."

CHAPTER 7

"What happened?" Rhys asked as he reached up and Callan gently handed the animal to him.

"Someone cut the fence," Callan said with a snarl as he dismounted. "Found him hung up in it."

Rhys felt blood seep into his shirt as he carried the animal into the barn. He guessed the calf weighed less than a hundred pounds, but the slick blood made it difficult to maneuver and he was glad when Callan appeared next to him and tossed a horse blanket on the cement floor of the aisle and helped him gently put the calf down on it. Finn appeared with a cordless phone in his hand. He was pale as he dropped down to the floor next to them.

"How long till he gets here?" Callan asked.

"He's not coming. His office said he's booked all day."

Callan dropped his eyes and Finn crossed his arms as if in pain. "Did you tell them it was an emergency?" Rhys asked in growing irritation as they both just sat there.

"It won't matter. He won't come," Callan said dejectedly. He got up and went back to his horse. He reappeared seconds later, a rifle in his hand.

"No! No fucking way," Rhys snarled as he picked up the animal.

"Rhys," Finn said softly.

"Get the truck, Finn," Rhys ordered. When Finn didn't move Rhys yelled, "Get the god damn truck!"

Finn shifted his eyes to Callan, but Rhys wasn't sure if the other man gave his permission or not. Frankly, he didn't care. He started walking toward the front of the barn. Finn pulled the truck up and Rhys hurried to the bed of the truck. Callan appeared next to him.

"Give him to me," Callan said. Rhys hesitated, then passed him the calf so he could climb into the bed of the truck. Callan handed the animal back to him, then picked up the rifle from where he'd leaned it against the truck. He gave the gun to Finn and said, "Can you get the herd back and start on the fence? Only a few had crossed it when I found him," Callan said, motioning to the calf.

Finn nodded and lifted his gaze to Rhys'. Rhys could see the regret in the other man's eyes, but he forced himself to focus on the too quiet animal in his arms.

Rhys had to admire Callan's driving skills because they managed to make it to the vet's office on the outskirts of town within ten minutes, a trip that had taken much longer when Rhys had hitched his way out to the ranch two days ago.

The vet's office was a ramshackle building with a small shed along the side and some dog kennels in back. There were only a few cars parked in the lot and Callan didn't hesitate to pull right up to the front door, barely missing a little old lady that came out of the entrance, a small brown dog in her arms.

"Sorry ma'am," Callan mumbled as he took the calf from Rhys so he could climb out of the bed of the truck. The woman opened her mouth in surprise as he and Callan brushed past her and he guessed that the sight of the calf along with the blood staining Rhys' shirt weren't an everyday occurrence.

Rhys opened the door and Callan hurried in, his voice bellowing, "Need some help here." He'd expected people to jump into action, but he was sorely mistaken. Two patrons sat in the lobby, their eyes widening at the sight. A young woman - a technician Rhys guessed - started to come around to the lobby but the woman behind the desk stopped her with a sharp look, then turned her frosty gaze on Callan.

"Mr. Bale, as I explained to your...associate," the receptionist said in distaste. "Dr. Sanders is completely booked up."

Rhys had gone completely still when the woman had referred to Finn that way and the disgust actually had him reaching over the counter towards her when Callan used his body to stop him. "Are you for real?" he snapped at the woman. He glanced at the technician standing next to the woman, but she stood there mutely, her eyes wide and unsure.

Rhys started to go to the side door when it opened and an older man in a white coat stepped out, his thinning, silver hair slicked off to one side. His eyes narrowed when they settled on Callan.

"Is there a problem here, Anita?" he asked the receptionist, though his smug gaze never left Callan's.

"I've informed Mr. Bale that you aren't available," the woman said snidely.

"Dr. Sanders," Rhys said. The man's haughty gaze settled on him. "As you can see, this animal is badly hurt-"

"Mrs. Parsons, why don't you come on back?" Dr. Sanders said to one of the women sitting in the lobby, though his eyes remained on Rhys.

"Rhys, let's go," Callan said coldly, clearly unsurprised by the reception they were getting.

"Jesus, are you fucking kidding me?" Rhys shouted. "You'd actually let this animal die just to spite someone you don't like?"

"Rhys!"

Rhys turned to look at Callan, frustrated that he wasn't doing anything. But then reality set in – what was happening wasn't new for him or for Finn. They lived this everyday – had been living it for two years.

"Mr. Bale?"

All heads turned to see the old woman from the parking lot

standing just inside the doorway, the brown dog cradled lovingly in her withered arms. "You're Dolly's nephew, right?" she asked Callan.

He nodded stiffly, clearly readying himself for another attack.

"There's a new vet who just moved to town last week. He's not set up or anything yet, but maybe he can help you. Dr. Winters. He's at the old Humphries place. You know it?" she asked.

Callan was already moving towards the door. "Yes ma'am. Thank you."

"You go on now and I'll give him a call to let him know you're coming," she ordered as she marched up to the reception desk and stood on her tip toes so she could reach the phone. She tucked her dog under one arm, then grabbed the whole phone with her free hand and pulled it up on the counter so she could dial.

"Mrs. Greene," the vet began, but she quelled him with a sharp look and he snapped his mouth shut.

"Wendy, be a dear and find me the number for Dr. Winters," she said sweetly to the technician who quickly moved to do her bidding.

Rhys followed Callan out the door and took the calf from him once he was once again settled in the bed of the truck. "Greene? Any relation to-"

Callan nodded stiffly. "She's Hunter Greene's grandmother."

~

"You do it," Rhys muttered as he resisted the urge to clap his hands over his ears to drown out the sound of the screaming baby. The last thing he'd expected when they arrived at Dr. Dane Winters' house was to be handed a car seat with a sleeping baby girl in it.

"I don't know the first thing about kids," Callan snapped.

"And you think I do?" Rhys shot back as he used his boot to rock the car seat back and forth gently in hopes it would put the kid out again like she'd been when they'd gotten here.

Dane Winters hadn't been anything like they'd expected, but Rhys had been relieved when the man had greeted them in the driveway and led them to a small building behind the old Victorian style house. Rhys hadn't even noticed the vet was carrying the baby until he'd asked Rhys and Callan to watch the child while he got to work on the calf. Callan had managed to remember to wash his hands before he grabbed the car seat and they'd headed to the waiting room, or what Rhys guessed would someday be the waiting room since a couple of plastic, foldable chairs stuffed in the corner amidst a sea of boxes probably didn't really count.

"He said to give her the bottle if she got fussy," Callan said as he carefully searched the diaper bag that somehow Rhys had also missed. "Here," he said, shoving the bag at him.

"What the hell are all these pockets for?" Rhys mumbled as he looked through the contents and finally found what he assumed was the baby's milk.

Callan was trying to work the car seat straps free and asked, "Is there a towel or blanket in there or something?"

Callan rolled up the bloodied sleeves of his work shirt and took the fluffy blanket with pink and grey elephants on it that Rhys handed him and draped it over his shoulder so the baby wouldn't come into contact with the dried blood on his shirt. It took him a couple of minutes to maneuver the squirming baby free of the seat, but he managed to get her cradled against his blanket-covered chest. Rhys handed him the bottle and nearly shouted for joy when the baby instantly started sucking on it and the room was drenched in blessed silence.

"Thank God," he said as he lowered the diaper bag to the floor. He watched in amusement as the big man stood awkwardly as the baby stared up at him while she drank from the bottle.

"Looks good on you," Rhys said with a smile, then nearly laughed at the horrified expression that crossed Callan's face. "What, you never thought about kids before?"

"No," Callan managed to choke out.

Rhys leaned back in his chair. "Too bad Finn isn't here. I bet he'd be a natural at this." A flash of longing went through Callan's eyes before he turned away and walked a few steps to the window. "Heard he gave his notice," Rhys probed. Callan tensed slightly, but didn't respond otherwise. "Probably for the best. Once he's gone, all your problems go with him, right?" Still nothing.

Several minutes passed before Callan turned around and carried the now sleeping baby and gently placed her in the carrier. He didn't bother with the straps, but he did turn the carrier around so that the baby was facing away from them. Then, without warning, Callan grabbed Rhys by the collar, dragged him out of the chair and slammed him back against the wall.

"You say shit like that to me again about Finn and we're going to have a problem!" he said harshly, though Rhys suspected he kept his voice down for the baby's benefit.

"You going to fire me again, big guy?" Rhys said lightly though his body was drawn tight with the adrenaline rush of having Callan's body pressed against his, his big hand wrapped around Rhys' throat. Rhys dared to drop his hand over the erection he suspected Callan was fighting and he wasn't disappointed. "Or you going to do some-thing else to me?" he drawled.

The need to drive this man to lose control was overwhelming and he actually stopped breathing when Callan's eyes dropped to his mouth. Rhys stroked Callan through his pants and was rewarded with Callan grabbing his hand. But Callan didn't stop him. He just covered Rhys' fingers with his own, following the motion as Rhys rubbed his hardness over and over.

The sound of footsteps had Callan abruptly stepping away from Rhys and all the air rushed out of his lungs at once making him light headed.

"Mr. Bale," the vet said as he came into the waiting room. His eyes darted from Callan to Rhys as he went to the baby's car seat and leaned down to check her.

"Call me Callan," Callan managed to get out, his voice sounding a bit shaky.

"The calf is doing as well as can be expected, considering the circumstances. I got him stitched up and the fluids are helping to ease the shock. He's not out of the woods, but I think you guys got to him in time," Dr. Winters said as he lifted the car seat from the floor and placed it on one of the chairs. His eyes softened as he gazed adoringly at the baby. Rhys guessed the man to be in his early forties and just the slightest hint of silver glinted in his chocolate brown hair. Dark brown eyes melted as he watched the baby snuggle further into the car seat.

"Thank you, Dr. Winters," Callan said.

"It's Dane, please," the man responded. "Thanks for keeping an eye on Emma for me. We're still trying to get settled and I haven't had a chance to find someone to help me watch her yet."

"We just appreciate you taking a look at the calf," Rhys interjected as he reached out to shake Dane's hand.

"Not a problem. I haven't decided if I'm going to start a new practice right away, but I'm glad I was able to help."

"Did you and your wife just move here?" Rhys asked.

"Yes, from L.A. But I'm not married anymore. I lost my husband four months ago," Dane said matter-of-factly.

"Sorry," Rhys managed to say, though truth be told, he was more than caught off guard by learning the man was gay.

"How old is she?" he heard Callan ask.

"Six months," Dane said, a slight unevenness in his tone. He forced a smile to his lips and said, "I'd like to keep the calf overnight if that's all right with you."

Callan nodded, then pulled out his wallet. "How much do I owe you, Doctor?" Rhys watched as Callan nervously counted the few bills he had in his wallet.

The vet must have noticed too because he said, "Actually, I have a proposition for you. Mrs. Greene tells me you occasionally board horses and I was wondering if you might be willing to do a little trade?"

Rhys knew from talking with Finn that the only horses on Callan's property were his own so if he did board them at one time, Rhys guessed the owners had removed them after Finn's run in with Hunter Greene and his father.

"You need a horse boarded?" Callan asked somewhat suspiciously.

Dane nodded. "My husband inherited this property and everything that came with it when his aunt and uncle died last year in a car accident. Kirby's a nice, quiet horse and I've decided to keep him for Emma," he said, motioning towards his daughter who was blessedly still asleep. "The barn here is in pretty bad shape so I'm having it torn down next week and rebuilt. I hate for Kirby not to have a place to escape from the heat. What do you say?"

Rhys wanted to shove Callan for the dark look he was giving the vet. Trust was clearly something Callan had lost somewhere along the way and a man like him wouldn't look too kindly on charity or pity. He finally relaxed and reached out his hand to the vet. "Sounds good. I can pick Kirby up tomorrow when I come get the calf," Callan offered.

"That'd be great. Thank you," Dane said, shaking Callan's hand, a wide smile on his kind face. They followed Dane out of the building and gave him a wave as he carried his daughter into the house.

"You think he has any idea what a fucked up town he moved to?" Rhys asked.

Callan grunted and went to the truck. Rhys climbed into the passenger side and within minutes they were back on the dirt road leading to the ranch. Callan seemed edgy and tense as his fingers drummed on the steering wheel, but Rhys was too worn out to try and draw the moody man into conversation.

Suddenly Callan slammed on the brakes and threw the truck into park, the motion jerking Rhys forward.

"What the fu-" Rhys said an instant before Callan reached across the seat, grabbed him by the neck and slammed his mouth down on his. The pleasure that surged through Rhys was instantaneous, but his entire body lit up like a brush fire when Callan's tongue licked across his lips, seeking entry. Before he could even react though, Callan was pulling back, but he didn't let go of Rhys' neck.

Callan dropped his forehead to Rhys' and the combined sounds of their harsh breathing actually seemed louder than the idling truck.

Rhys' hand had somehow found its way to Callan's thigh and the muscles were tight beneath his palm as Callan seemed to try to regain his control. Any second now he knew Callan would pull away from him, put the truck in gear and they'd both try to forget this had happened – they'd just chalk it up to the traumatic events of the day.

But Callan didn't pull back, didn't release him. Instead, those lips found their way back to his and Callan kissed him softly, almost reverently. Rhys knew it was crazy, but Callan's sudden gentleness somehow seemed like an apology. Rhys opened to Callan's seeking tongue and groaned in satisfaction as his mouth was explored – worshipped. Callan kissed him like he had all the time in the world and Rhys felt heat spread from his belly to his groin as the need intensified. He pushed his own tongue into Callan's mouth to get a taste, then used his weight to press Callan back against the seat. It took only a little maneuvering before he was sprawled on top of the bigger man. He grabbed Callan's arms to pin them above his head so he could plunder Callan's mouth exactly the way he wanted to, but the second his fingers closed around Callan's wrists, the other man froze and then it was like his whole body shut down.

Rhys pulled back slightly and saw that Callan had his eyes squeezed shut and his face was clenched as if in pain. "Callan," Rhys said gently as he carefully released his hold on Callan's wrists. "Callan, look at me," Rhys ordered softly as a surge of realization went through him. The man had been enjoying what was happening between them until Rhys had taken control – had restrained him. But instead of lashing out in fear or anger, Callan had shut down, turned off.

Worry shot through Rhys at the complete lack of response. "Callan, please, open your eyes, baby. You're safe," he said as he stroked his fingers along Callan's tight jaw. The man's teeth were gnashed together so hard Rhys was afraid he'd hurt himself. Rhys carefully lifted all his weight off of Callan, but continued to stroke him gently. Finally, he felt some of the tension in Callan's body ease and his eyes opened and focused on Rhys. Something inside the other man seemed to switch back on and he pushed up, then grabbed for the door handle and stumbled out of the truck. Rhys followed him out and watched him suck in deep gasps of air as he fought to regain control of himself.

~

What the fuck had he done? Callan tried to drag in air, but his chest hurt so bad that every breath seemed to just whistle uselessly through him. He felt a warm palm settle over his back and rub in large circles, but the touch made things worse so he pulled away. Feeling Rhys' knowing gaze burning into him, Callan took several steps away from the truck and was glad when he didn't hear Rhys follow. He bent over and closed his eyes and forced himself to focus only on taking in a breath and releasing it. Then another. He wasn't sure how long he did it for but the stabbing pain finally went away, only to be replaced by a knot of shame low in his belly. Not only had he just outed himself, he'd done it with a man he knew Finn was interested in. Worse yet, Rhys had witnessed his secret shame.

"You okay?" he heard Rhys ask from just behind him. The pity in the other man's voice was proof that Rhys suspected what had caused Callan's reaction. Callan managed a quick nod, then pushed past the other man and headed back to the truck.

"We should get moving. Finn's probably got his hands full with the fence."

"We need to talk about what just happened, Callan," he heard Rhys say.

Callan climbed into the truck and kept his eyes straight ahead as Rhys returned to the passenger seat. The second the door closed he put the truck in gear and hit the gas. He was glad when Rhys didn't press him further. Pulling the truck in front of the barn, he put it in park and turned it off, but didn't get out. Rhys sat quietly next to him as if waiting for Callan's next move.

"He can't find out about this," Callan said quietly. He actually felt sorry for Rhys when he saw the indecision flicker across the other man's features.

"He has a right to know," Rhys responded.

Callan sighed, then looked out the window at the property. God, the place was falling apart. Everywhere he looked he saw something that needed attention and he suddenly felt overwhelmed by it all. He was fighting a losing battle and he knew it and there was absolutely no way out.

"I'm so tired, Rhys," he admitted as he felt the sting of tears. "So fucking tired."

~

*R*hys felt the overwhelming urge to pull Callan against him as he saw all the fight leave the other man's body. He reached out and skimmed his fingers through the soft hair above Callan's right ear. His cowboy hat had somehow ended up in the backseat of the truck during their encounter earlier and Rhys realized he'd never seen Callan without it.

Callan actually seemed to press into Rhys' touch and then he leaned his head back against the seat as Rhys continued to pet him. "Thank you for what you did today for the calf. Sometimes it's too much, you know?" he said as he turned his eyes on Rhys.

"What is?" Rhys asked gently.

"Fighting. We've been doing it for so long that sometimes it's just easier not to I guess." Callan closed his eyes again. "If you tell him, you know he'll never go."

Rhys dropped his hand from Callan's hair. Everything in his gut told him it was wrong to be a part of Callan's lie, but it wasn't his truth to tell, was it?

"If Finn thinks he has any chance at a life with me, he'll never move on. He'll stay here in a town that punishes him because he refuses to be someone he's not," Callan reminded him.

"*Does* he have a chance with you?" Rhys held his breath waiting for the answer, not sure why it really mattered and not sure what he wanted that answer to actually be.

Callan didn't respond and Rhys wasn't surprised. Whatever secrets this man held, they ran deep. A quick make-out session wasn't going to get him to magically open up to Rhys.

"I won't tell him," Rhys finally said. "But what happened between us can't happen again. I won't hurt him," he declared as he reached for the door handle of the truck. He hesitated, then glanced back at Callan. "Maybe fighting wouldn't be so hard if you let Finn stand beside you instead of behind you. He's not a child, Callan. And I think you'd be a fucking fool to let him go."

CHAPTER 8

*F*inn stared at the ceiling above him and tried to quell the knot of anxiety in his gut. The day had sucked from beginning to end and the only brief, bright spot had been when Rhys had kissed him. And then Finn had fucked that up too. Any hope that Rhys might have forgiven him the transgression had disintegrated upon Cal and Rhys' arrival to help him fix the fence. Both men had kept their distance from him and Rhys had only offered clipped, one word responses when he asked how the calf was doing. He'd hoped that once they got back to the house things might change, but Rhys had fixed himself a sandwich and then disappeared into his room. Finn hadn't bothered with food since he wasn't sure he could keep anything down anyway, so he'd climbed into the shower, then crawled into bed. That was three hours ago and he was no closer to falling asleep.

How had he messed things up so badly? He'd only known Rhys for a couple of days but it somehow felt longer. And it shouldn't matter what went on between him and Rhys going forward because Finn was leaving. Even if he weren't, Rhys was going back to Chicago as soon as his parole was done. Any relationship he might have with the man would be purely physical and he knew in his gut that it wouldn't be enough. He'd be in the same position he was in with Cal – wanting someone who didn't want him back. Pain lanced through him at the prospect and he began to fear that he'd waited too long to walk away.

~

*R*hys heard his already ajar door being opened and he tensed, though not because he was worried about a stranger coming into his room in the middle of the night. He'd debated locking the door when he'd gone to bed, but even just the thought of being in a completely closed off room had brought back the old anxiety from being locked in his jail cell for 23 hours a day for two years and he couldn't bring himself to do it. He hadn't even been able to close the door all the way. Ignoring Finn for the rest of the day was supposed to have been the first step in his plan to distance himself from the two men that were wreaking havoc on his senses, but apparently the other man hadn't gotten the message. Rhys' back was to the door so he had to glance over his shoulder to see the slumped form standing next to the bed.

"Finn-" he began, steeling himself to send the man away.

"Please, Rhys," he heard Finn whisper brokenly. "I just need to sleep," he said, his voice pleading.

Rhys tried to stiffen his resolve, but an image of Finn smiling at him when he'd picked him up in the truck that first day went through his head. Rhys pulled the covers back and Finn went around to the other side of the bed and crawled in, putting his back to Rhys. It wasn't a big bed, but Finn pressed himself up along the edge of the mattress, putting as much distance between him and Rhys as he could and Rhys wondered if he did it because that was what he wanted or it was because he thought it was what Rhys wanted.

Rhys let out a soft curse, then reached out his arm and grabbed Finn by the waist and dragged him back against his chest. Finn gasped as Rhys' thickening cock settled against his ass, the thin fabric of Finn's pajama bottoms and Rhys' briefs doing little to inhibit the contact. He felt Finn's hand close over his own. God, it would be so easy to roll Finn on his back and take him. He knew from the heavy breathing and tight body pressed against his that Finn wanted him just as badly. And if today hadn't happened then he'd probably already have his dick pressed deep inside the other man as he watched him come apart around him. But seeing firsthand what Finn would suffer through if he stayed in this place had him saying, "Go to sleep, Finn," instead. Rhys had never claimed to be an honorable man, but he'd be damned if he was going to add himself to the long list of people fucking with Finn's emotions.

~

*R*hys tinkered with the manure spreader as the early morning heat burned into his back. It was barely eight o'clock in the morning and he felt like he'd lost half his body weight through his sweat. He'd never understood why Callan and Finn continued to wear long sleeved shirts in the blazing sun, but as his sunburned skin flamed where his T-shirt sleeve grazed the sensitive flesh, he started to realize he was the one on the losing end of that particular argument. The cowboy hat that always seemed like an accessory before was now on the top of his wish list.

He climbed out of the foul-smelling spreader and threw the tools in the ramshackle box that Finn called the toolbox. Heading back to the barn, he saw Finn cleaning the last stall. This had become their routine over the last few days. Callan would be out most of the day riding the fence line and Finn would be taking care of the horses. Rhys had taken it upon himself to start fixing the many things that were broken around the place including repairing siding, patching holes in the roof of the barn, mending the paddock fences, and now fixing the spreader. Neither of them talked to one another throughout the day unless it was absolutely necessary and when the work day ended, Callan would disappear up to the main house to work on the books while Finn wandered off on one of his many walks. Rhys managed to watch the news or an old sitcom as he forced down some tasteless food before crawling into bed. The hardest part of his day came when Finn crawled into the bed next to him.

It was something he should have stopped after the first night he dragged Finn against him and held him all night, but each time Finn showed up, he remained silent and waited until that warm, lean body was pressed against his, filling places Rhys hadn't realized were empty. His arm would go around Finn before he could even think better of it and he'd wait for the desire in his body to settle enough that sleep could claim him. And for the first time in a long time, he slept through the night. Finn was always gone the next morning before he awoke and it was just something that *was* and they never talked about it.

"Finn, I need a ride to the hardware store," he said as he stopped outside the stall Finn was working on.

"Keys are in the truck," came the clipped response.

Rhys bit back his frustration. "You have to drive me."

Finn stopped cleaning and looked up. "It's not far. You won't get lost," he said.

"I don't have a license," Rhys finally admitted. "And I'm not about to risk my parole by driving without one."

Finn fidgeted. "Just leave the spreader. We've been doing fine without it," he said lamely.

"Yeah, well 'we' will be me when you leave and I don't want to keep busting my ass hauling shit out to the field when there's a perfectly good piece of machinery capable of doing the job." Finn stiffened at the reminder that he was leaving and then anger flashed across his features as he shoved past the wheelbarrow and headed towards the truck. Rhys felt a stirring of lust at finally getting some kind of a response out of the other man who'd been on autopilot for the better part of a week now.

The trip to town was made in silence which had Rhys' frustration ticking up with each mile that flew past. Finn pulled to a stop in front of the hardware store and turned the truck off, then just sat there.

"You're coming in with me," Rhys snapped as he reached for the door handle.

"No, I'm not," Finn said quietly, his eyes dropping to his hands as a man walked past the front of a truck, his beady eyes fastened on Finn.

Rhys leaned over and grabbed Finn's arm. "Get your fucking ass out of the truck right now!" Rhys got out of the truck and was satisfied to see Finn following his order.

"Why are you doing this?" Finn whispered.

Rhys didn't answer as he headed into the store, Finn trailing a few steps behind. He marched past the portly clerk behind the counter who'd started to greet them, but fell silent when his eyes settled on Finn. It took Rhys only minutes to find the screws he needed and then they were making their way back to the front of the store. He dropped the screws on the counter.

The clerk ignored Rhys and stared at Finn, his face ruddy with anger. "I told you you weren't welcome in my store anymore," he nearly spit out.

"Hey!" Rhys said sharply, forcing the clerk's gaze to his face. "You've got something to say, you say it to me!"

The man glanced back at Finn with disgust, then settled his eyes on Rhys and said, "I don't want his kind in my store."

White hot rage went through Rhys. "His kind?" he asked, his voice low.

"Rhys," Finn said from behind him.

The clerk finally seemed to sense Rhys' anger because he fell silent and the sneer disappeared from his face as apprehension went through him.

"Tell me exactly what 'his kind' is," Rhys said.

"Rhys," Finn tried again.

"You mean guys who take it up the ass? Or guys who prefer sucking dick to pussy?" Rhys snarled. "What do hillbilly fucks like you call 'his kind' out here? Queer, fag? Or you got some fancy bible-ass term you hide behind like sinner or abomination?"

"Rhys, let's just go," Finn pleaded. Rhys turned and saw that the few customers in the store were all watching them now.

"Fucking cowards and hypocrites," Rhys quipped as he focused on each person who just stood there transfixed. "Well, guess what, you've got two fags invading your precious little town now," he said with a smile.

"Three," came another voice and Rhys hid a smile when Dane Winters appeared from one of the aisles, Emma cradled in one arm, a shopping basket in the other. He dropped the basket in front of the clerk and said, "I believe we're ready to check out now, Mr. Henry."

The clerk looked like he was about to have a heart attack, but he managed to start ringing up Dane's purchases. 'These too," Dane said as he pushed the screws Rhys had dropped on the counter forward. The clerk hesitated before finally taking them.

As he began bagging the items, Dane turned and smiled at Finn, then extended his hand. "Dane Winters," he said. Finn managed to stick out a shaky hand. Dane turned his attention to Rhys and began chatting as if there weren't half a dozen eyes staring at them in mute shock. "Thought I'd bring Emma by this afternoon to check in on Kirby. How's he doing?"

"He's good," Rhys said, his respect for this man skyrocketing.

"And the calf?" Dane asked as he handed the clerk his credit card.

"On the mend," Finn interjected. "Back out with his mama."

"Can you believe it, Mr. Henry?" Dane said. The clerk seemed caught off guard that Dane was speaking with him directly and stilled as he was about to run the credit card through. "Someone cut the fence on Mr. Bale's ranch and one of the little ones got caught up in the wire and nearly died."

The clerk was at a loss for words, so he just shook his head awkwardly.

Dane glanced around at the other customers, then turned his cool gaze back on Mr. Henry. "You know what else, Mr. Henry?"

Dane let his question hang there until the clerk finally managed to rasp out, "What?"

"It turns out your town's one vet isn't available to treat emergencies anymore. I guess Mrs. Parson's cat needed its yearly shots more than that calf needed saving. Damn shame your only other option is someone who likes sucking dick too," he said with a sad shake of his head as he took the bag from the clerk. "Oh, and Mr. Henry, would you please cancel the order I placed yesterday for the lumber for my new barn? I think I'll be taking my business elsewhere."

The clerk's mouth fell open at that and Rhys smiled as Dane pushed past him and left the store. Finn, still looking shell-shocked, followed the vet out the door.

"One last thing," Rhys said as he leaned over the counter and dropped his voice. "If Finn so much as gets a hangnail the next time he comes into this town…" Rhys let his words drop off and Mr. Henry went pale. He turned and nodded politely at the gawkers, then left.

~

*R*hys waited for the explosion he knew was coming. After he'd walked out of the store, Finn's furious gaze had pinned him, but the younger man had kept it together long enough to say his goodbyes to Dane. Rhys had settled in the passenger seat and waited for the shouting to commence, but Finn had remained silent. But when Rhys had mentioned he'd needed to stop and get a hat and a couple of shirts, Finn had completely ignored him and steered the truck back to the ranch.

The truck flew up the dirt road leading to the ranch, dust and gravel shooting up in its wake. The vehicle came within inches of slamming into the side of the barn before Finn smashed down the brakes and the truck lurched to a halt. Finn barreled out the door and stormed into the barn. Rhys trailed after him and leaned against one of the stall doors as he waited for Finn to unleash his fury.

"You had no fucking right," Finn said bitterly, his back to Rhys. Rhys remained silent which seemed to piss Finn off further. He swung around, stalked up to Rhys and threw a punch. Rhys had been expecting it though, and easily caught the fist aimed at his face. He shoved Finn back up against the door and held him there, pinning his wrists to the door. But Finn wasn't about to submit and head butted Rhys. The glancing blow had him seeing stars, but he managed to maintain his hold on Finn.

"Stop it!" he snarled.

"Go to hell!"

"Rhys." Callan's voice came from somewhere behind him and Rhys chuckled harshly, but kept his eyes on Finn.

"Running to his rescue again, Callan?" Rhys said and he felt Finn lurch against him once more as he tried to escape.

"What's going on?" Callan asked. Rhys was amazed the other man hadn't pulled him off Finn. Finn seemed caught off guard by Callan's lack of action too because he stilled in Rhys' grip.

"You couldn't just let it go, could you Rhys?" Finn said snidely. "A couple more weeks and it all would have been over, but no, you had to play the big hero! Do you really think you made everything better? That you changed anything at all?" Finn shouted. "You get to leave in six months. He doesn't," Finn said, his eyes shifting behind Rhys, presumably to Callan. "Now they'll never stop coming at him!"

"Finn," Callan began.

"No! He had no right. It was my fight!" Finn said.

"Not if you stop fucking fighting, it's not!" Rhys responded sharply.

"My choice! Not yours!" Finn yelled and shoved Rhys hard. Rhys let him go and Finn pushed past him and stormed out of the barn. Rhys slammed his hand into the wood and closed his eyes as the stinging pain shot through him.

He felt Callan behind him, then felt the other man take his hand and examine it. "Talk to me, Rhys. Tell me what went down."

Rhys pulled his hand free. He gave Callan a quick rundown of what had transpired in town.

"You did the right thing," Callan observed. "He'll see that."

"Doesn't matter. I'm done with this shit," Rhys said, but Callan grabbed him by the arm, preventing his escape.

"Come take a ride with me. It'll help you cool down and I could use a hand checking the fences." Callan's touch strong and soothing and Rhys wished he could sink into the man for just a minute and absorb some of his strength. He settled for a quick nod and followed Callan out to the pasture to get the horses.

CHAPTER 9

Finn went on instant alert when he heard the sound of a car approaching. He was in the process of bringing the horses in for their evening feeding and for the first time in the hours since his blowout with Rhys, he'd finally started to relax. But the possible new threat had him scurrying to the tack room to get the rifle Cal had left him for exactly such a scenario. He checked to make sure the gun was loaded, then went to the front of the barn. Relief went through him at the sight of Dane Winters getting his baby from the car seat out of the back seat of his SUV.

"Hello again," Dane said as he slung a diaper bag over his shoulder and closed the door. "That some kind of Montana greeting?" he asked as he glanced at the rifle Finn was still holding, the barrel pointed at the ground.

Finn finally remembered the gun and said, "No, sorry," and he quickly returned the gun to the tack room. He went back to Dane who was busy showing his daughter the few horses that Finn had gotten into their stalls. The baby made a few gurgling sounds and waved her hands and a huge grin spilled across Dane's handsome features. Cal had mentioned that Dane would be boarding his horse at the ranch for a while, but beyond that Finn knew nothing about the man. Well, he supposed that wasn't true anymore since Dane's little show of support had revealed a pretty important detail about the other man's life.

"We just wanted to come and feed Kirby a couple of carrots if that's okay," Dane said as he repositioned the baby so she was nestled in the crook of one arm.

"He's still outside. I'll go get him," Finn offered.

"We'll go with you if it's not too far of a walk," Dane said with a smile as he tickled the baby's chubby cheeks with one of his big fingers. The sight set off a longing inside of Finn that he hadn't known he had. When he'd brought up the issue of having kids someday to Cal the night he'd given his notice, the words had been spoken to bolster his argument and represented some far off time in his life. But seeing the open love this man – this gay man – had for his child had Finn realizing it was something he really did want.

"Um, it's just up the hill. Not far," Finn managed to say.

"Great."

Dane fell in step behind him, then said, "Would you like to hold her?"

Finn realized he must have been staring at the baby more than he realized and he quickly said, "No, my hands are dirty. And I've never been around a baby before."

"Don't worry Finn, you won't break her. I was scared to death the first time a nurse handed her to me, but it only took about ten seconds to realize that holding her is one of the easiest things I'll ever do."

Finn nodded his head and tried to wipe some of the dust off his hands by running them down his pants. He held his arms the way he'd seen Dane doing when he first carried her into the barn and the man carefully placed her in them.

An overwhelming rush of insecurity went through him at the feeling of the warm, squirmy body in his hands. He tried to hand her back but Dane said, "You're doing fine. Just give it a second." He pulled the baby closer to his chest and then found himself staring into the purest, brightest blue eyes he'd ever seen.

"Oh God," he whispered as the baby watched him with complete trust.

"What'd I tell you?" Dane said with a laugh as he began walking. Finn took careful, even steps as he followed the other man out towards the pasture.

"You expecting trouble after this afternoon?" Dane asked.

Finn looked up in confusion. "What?"

"The gun," Dane reminded him.

"Oh, uh...we don't get a lot of visitors out here," he said lamely. When Dane didn't say anything, Finn floundered and said, "I'm sorry for the position Rhys put you in today. He shouldn't have pulled you into my fight."

Dane actually stopped and looked at Finn, his eyes cool and calm. "I didn't do it for you, Finn. Although I'm glad if it helped in any way," Dane said. "No, I did it for my daughter," he finished, then started walking again.

"I don't understand."

"I want Emma to grow up in a world where she's free to be whomever she was meant to be. To love whomever she wants to love. How can I expect people around me to change if I don't ask them to – expect them to? I hope she never has to face the same battles you and I do, but if she does, I want her to know her father was there from the start, trying to make a better place for her. Maybe then she won't have to fight quite so hard or quite so long."

Finn fell silent at Dane's words.

"Hey Kirby, old man," Dane said as the brown and white Pinto nickered in greeting and trotted up to the fence. "Look Emma," Dane said as he took his daughter back and showed her the big horse who hung his nearly all white face over the fence. Finn snapped a lead on Kirby and West who was the only other horse in the pasture and began leading them back to the barn. Dane's words kept resonating through his head as he put West away and then tied Kirby in cross ties.

"You okay?" Dane asked as he fished out a carrot from the diaper bag and fed it to Kirby.

"Yeah," Finn muttered, though his mind was already on how he'd ever get Rhys to forgive him for his earlier behavior. It could be that anything he said would be too little, too late.

～

*R*hys collapsed on the bed after his shower and wished to hell he could just order a pizza because he was too tired to have to stand in the kitchen for the five minutes it would take to slap some meat and cheese between two slices of bread. At least his ass wasn't hurting as much as his body started adjusting to sitting in a saddle for extended periods of time. The view hadn't hurt either. Callan on a horse was something to behold. He'd even been wearing the old style leather chaps that had a nice cutout emphasizing the perfection that was his ass. All sorts of dirty images of Callan in chaps sans jeans had flitted through his mind, though he'd tried to ignore the fact that Finn was also front and center in the naughty little show he'd had going on in his head.

He and Callan hadn't seen Finn once they got back from checking the fences and Finn's bedroom door was closed so Rhys was pretty sure he'd be spending the night alone for the first time in well over a week. Rhys slipped under the covers and turned off the light on the nightstand. Callan had been right about the ride. It had given him time to cool off. What's more, Callan hadn't given him the lecture he'd expected about needing to be more careful with Finn.

In fact, Callan hadn't said a word other than to give him instructions on how to improve his seat so the ride would be more comfortable for him. There'd even been a point where Callan had stopped, dismounted and checked the girth on Rhys' saddle because he was concerned it had been too loose. The man's big hand had closed around Rhys' leg to move it out of the way as he checked the fastenings – a move that was entirely innocent in nature but had the same effect as Callan stroking over his cock with his tongue. It had felt good to have someone worry about him, even if it was just for a second and was more about keeping an employee safe rather than protecting a loved one from danger. Jesus, where had that word come from?

Rhys' disturbing thoughts were interrupted by the tell-tale sound of his door being pushed further open. His back was to the door so he did what he always did – threw back the covers and waited. At some point having Finn in his arms had become an expectation rather than a burden and even though he fought his body's desire until the blackness of sleep claimed him, he still welcomed the feel of the other man settling against him. As angry and frustrated as he still was with Finn, he was glad that at least this ritual would continue for the foreseeable future.

Rhys waited as Finn got under the covers, but was surprised when, instead of turning away from Rhys, Finn crawled across the bed and then pushed Rhys onto his back. Before he could even question the new position, Finn was leaning down and sealing his mouth over Rhys'. Finn's sweet taste flooded his mouth as the young man's tongue swept over every crevice and surface, then glided over Rhys' tongue. Finn's weight settled down on Rhys' chest as he continued his claiming of Rhys' lips, then that hot mouth was scorching a path down Rhys' neck. He managed to grab Finn by the shoulders and pull him up. "Finn, wait-"

"I don't want to wait anymore," Finn whispered. "I've been waiting my whole life for something that's right in front of me," he said before kissing Rhys again. Rhys knew he should stop this, that Finn belonged in another set of more capable arms, but he couldn't force himself to release the grip he had on Finn's upper arms. He gave up the battle and shifted so that he was laying on top of Finn. He let Finn have one more taste of him, then he took control of the kiss.

~

*F*inn wanted to cry in relief when he felt Rhys' weight cover him. When he'd climbed out of his own bed, he'd intended to crawl into Rhys' and beg for forgiveness, but as soon as he saw the other man lying under the covers, all the need he had pent up inside him spilled over and the only thing he'd wanted was to get his lips on Rhys and show him with his body how grateful he was for everything Rhys had given him. He knew the end result would be the same – he'd be alone when it was all over. But he would take what he could get and store the memory of being with this beautiful man away in a quiet part of his mind where he could get to it when he needed to remember why he'd made the choices he had.

Finn moaned as Rhys took control of every part of his mind and body. Warm, silky lips explored his mouth as blunt fingers stroked his chest and sides. His skin itched and tingled all over as the slight matting of hair on Rhys' wide chest brushed his hot skin. Rhys left nothing untouched as he worked his mouth down Finn's neck, whispering against his skin what he wanted to do to him. Finn tried to reach down to give his cock some much needed relief, but Rhys grabbed his hand and forced it above his head. "Grab the headboard," Rhys ordered as he moved Finn's other hand to join the first. Finn let out a rush of air at the command in Rhys' voice, but he did as he was told. The praise and appreciation in Rhys' gaze was worth it.

"Have you ever been with a man?" Rhys asked him as he pushed Finn's pajama bottoms down and trailed his fingers over Finn's painfully hard erection. Embarrassment flooded Finn's features as he shook his head.

"I'm going to take the edge off, Finn, because I want to explore every inch of this beautiful body before you get inside me," he said as he quickly worked his own underwear off, giving Finn his first sight of the long, thick hard cock that he'd been dreaming of since the day he'd stopped to give the man a ride to the ranch.

Finn stiffened at that. "I thought-"

"I want to be the first man you fuck, Finn. I want you to know what it will feel like for whatever man is lucky enough to take you someday."

Finn didn't get a chance to protest or even question Rhys' last statement because Rhys was kissing him again and all other thoughts fled as Rhys worked his way down Finn's body until he was settled between his legs. Rhys stripped off the pajama bottoms Finn was wearing, but Finn got no other warning before his dick was engulfed in white-hot wetness. He shouted as Rhys sucked him down until his nose was pressed against the rough hair of Finn's groin.

"Fuck!" Finn shouted as he pushed up into Rhys' lush mouth and grabbed him by the hair to hold him in place as he fucked into the overwhelming heat that surrounded him. Rhys began bobbing up and down on him, occasionally stopping only to dribble saliva along his length to smooth out his stroking. The pace Rhys set was ruthless and Finn could only hold on for the ride as his orgasm slammed into him and his seed spurted down Rhys' throat. The pleasure was so intense that it almost hurt and he dropped back onto the bed as Rhys continued to milk every last drop from him. A warm, tingling sensation passed along all his nerve endings and he closed his eyes as his body relaxed into the mattress.

Rhys crawled back up his body and settled over him once more as he kissed Finn over and over, long and hard, slow and soft, deep, shallow. It didn't matter to Finn, as long as the man kept up the contact. He tasted himself on Rhys' tongue and he languished at how forbidden it felt, yet so natural at the same time. He couldn't wait to see if Rhys had a similar flavor.

"What are you thinking that has that smile on your face?" Rhys said with a soft grin as he kissed the side of Finn's mouth.

"I'm wondering if you taste like me."

Rhys froze at that, then a sharp flash of lust went through his dark eyes and that mouth was hot on Finn's again, needy now as Rhys began working his body into a frenzy again.

~

*R*hys had told himself he would go slow the second time around, but Finn's comment about his taste had shredded the control he'd barely managed to hold on to when Finn shot down his throat. He gave Finn another hard kiss, then dragged his tongue down Finn's neck to the sensitive area above his collarbone. He pinched Finn's nipples with his fingers and smiled in satisfaction as

Finn moaned and arched beneath him. His cock was pressed against Finn's and Rhys reached between their bodies and rubbed their shafts together. Finn had recovered enough of his wits to start participating again and Rhys let Finn drag his mouth back down for another searing kiss. He let Finn roll him onto his back and spread his legs so Finn could lie between them. Those nimble fingers skimmed over his arms and chest, the pressure just enough to drive Rhys' need higher.

"Get me ready," Rhys said as he pulled his arm free from between their bodies and searched the nightstand drawer. Finn sat up on his knees and took the lube and condom that Rhys handed him, then lingered there, the small foil packet crunched up in his hand. He looked terrified. Rhys sat up and wrapped his arm around Finn's waist. "What's going on in that beautiful head of yours?" he asked between kisses. He was glad when Finn seemed to snap out of his funk and started returning each one.

"I don't want to hurt you," he whispered.

"Baby, nothing you do will hurt me. I swear." He took the condom from Finn's fist and opened it. Finn closed his eyes when Rhys gave him several long, slow pulls and Rhys wished he could drag this whole thing out just so he could enjoy the sight of Finn drowning in pleasure. But his own need was too great and he quickly rolled the condom down Finn's length.

Finn's eyes snapped open at the sound of the lube cap being clicked open and he stopped Rhys from pouring the sticky substance on his fingers. "Can I?" Finn asked shyly as he held out his own fingers. Rhys put a generous amount on them, then dribbled a small amount on Finn's cock and spread it around. He shifted so he could get on his hands and knees, but Finn stopped him again. "Can we be facing? I want to see you…"

A shudder went through Rhys at the reminder that this was so much more than a casual fuck. He couldn't even remember the last guy he'd been face to face with. Not even with his old partner, Tom, who he'd been exclusive with for nearly a year. It had always been quick and rough and rarely even in the bed. Fearing that he might not actually be able to get the word "yes" out, Rhys nodded and lowered himself to his back. He pulled his legs up and apart and watched as Finn reached out to expose his hole. And then Finn touched him and Rhys knew things would never be the same.

~

inn stared at Rhys' entrance, then reached out to run his thumb over it, needing to feel it without the lube. Rhys jumped at the contact and Finn looked up to make sure he was okay. The dark, raw passion staring back at him assured him he was good and the nearly purple head of Rhys' leaking cock took away any lingering doubt. He tested the wrinkly skin a few more times, then applied some of the lube. He worked his fingers in tiny circles around the opening and every couple of seconds, he'd dip the tip of one finger inside. Rhys began pushing against his fingers so he eased one in until it got past the first muscle. Rhys moaned and Finn closed his eyes at the feeling of Rhys' body clamping down on him. If it felt this tight on just his finger, how would he ever survive once his cock was all the way inside this beautiful man?

"Finn, please," he heard Rhys say and his eyes shot up to see the other man clenching his teeth together. Even though Finn was the one lacking experience, he suddenly realized how much power he had and a thrill went through him. His insecurities faded to the background as he used his free hand to pull one of Rhys' legs free of the death grip the man had on himself. He draped Rhys' leg against his shoulder, then motioned to Rhys to do the same with his other leg.

"Tell me how it feels," Finn whispered as he pulled his finger out, then pushed it back in.

"Good baby, so good. But I need more. Please."

Finn smiled at the nearly pleading sound in Rhys' tone. He worked a second finger in with the first and dragged them in and out in slow, tantalizing strokes, adding in a scissoring motion every once in a while that had Rhys squirming and moaning. Finn's intent had been to prolong this as long as he could, but he realized his body wasn't going to cooperate so he added a third finger.

71

"Rhys, I need you," he said as he pulled out and lined up his cock to the pulsing hole. He looked up to make sure Rhys was ready, but the other man seemed incapable of words and managed only a sharp nod as his fingers clenched in the bedding.

Finn pressed forward, his eyes alternating between watching the tip of his cock disappear into Rhys' body and looking up at Rhys to make sure he wasn't hurting him. But Rhys' head was pressed back, his eyes closed. With each push and pull motion that had him sinking further inside the hot channel, Rhys grunted.

"Rhys," Finn said uncertainly as he stilled.

"Fuck, don't stop!" Rhys cried out as he pushed his body down the bed trying to force Finn further inside. It was all Finn needed and he punched his hips forward and moaned when his balls slapped against Rhys' ass. The combined heat and pressure on his cock was nearly too much and he couldn't stop himself from pulling nearly all the way out and slamming back in again. Rhys' legs pressed down on Finn's shoulders as he began trying to lift himself to meet each thrust so Finn wrapped his arms around Finn's thighs to keep their bodies close as he sawed relentlessly in and out of Rhys.

"It's so good," he heard Rhys say and he nearly faltered when those luminous eyes opened and gazed back at him as Finn hammered into his welcoming body. He'd wanted to take Rhys from the front so he could see his eyes as he came, but he hadn't expected the over-whelming flood of emotion that would go through him. This strong, beautiful, sometimes crazy, always loyal man was letting Finn inside every part of him and it was nearly too much.

"Rhys," he whispered as tears stung his eyes. He leaned over and joined their mouths as he continued his thrusting and Rhys opened to him instantly and greeted his tongue. Arms wrapped around his back and Rhys' legs wrapped around his hips as he neared the end. He managed to get one of his hands between their hips and matched his strokes on the other man's cock with the brutal rhythm his body had set. He hoped to God he wasn't hurting Rhys with his thrusts, but he was too close to stop or slow. Pulling back from Rhys' mouth, he dropped his forehead down against Rhys' and gave up trying to keep his eyes open as the orgasm began to claim him. Two more hard jerks and he screamed in relief as his body let go and the seed shot from his pulsing cock. Rhys' fingers closed around the back of Finn's neck as he shouted his name, then shuddered and Finn felt his release coat his palm and splatter against their stomachs.

Finn's skin tingled and his muscles released and he suddenly felt boneless. His hand was still stuck between their sweaty bodies as Finn let all of his weight sag onto the hard body beneath his. Rhys' hot, heavy breath was against his neck and then there were light kisses along his shoulder as big hands closed around his ass and just held him there.

CHAPTER 10

*R*hys moaned at the feel of a slick tongue traveling up his cock before sucking gently on the flared head. He folded one arm under the back of his head so he could watch Finn go to town on his aching dick. Waking up with a very hot man wrapped around your body was one thing, but to have him worshipping your dick was a hundred times better. Even in his inexperience, Finn gave it his all. Just like last night.

Rhys had been fucked more times than he could count, had been the one doing the fucking even more often. But he'd never had something like last night happen. He'd never been in a place where sex became more than just a cock buried inside of him seeking release.

But last night had been a first because Finn hadn't held anything back, especially from his eyes. He doubted Finn even realized that his eyes were a window to every emotion the other man experienced. Last night Rhys had seen the whole range including fear, curiosity, confidence, power and awe. But it was seeing himself through Finn's eyes that had messed with his head and kept him up most of the night even as Finn lay wrapped around him, one leg thrown over Rhys' leg, another arm draped across his chest.

Finn had taken something as simple as sex and turned it into something more. For the first time in his life, Rhys had felt precious, wanted...needed. It was something Rhys couldn't imagine going without ever again, but that was exactly what would happen. He needed to remember that whatever he'd seen in Finn last night had been because it was his first time and he'd been overcome with the new sensations bombarding his body, not because he was feeling something for Rhys that he'd only felt for one other man - continued to feel for that man, Rhys reminded himself. Knowing that had been the only thing that kept Rhys from being the first man to have the pleasure of burying himself deep inside Finn's perfect body. It was something Finn should give to the man he loved, not the man who was a convenient placeholder.

Rhys pushed all thoughts from his head when Finn stopped torturing him and finally sucked him deep into his mouth. The younger man immediately gagged and pulled off, then gave Rhys a sheepish smile as he tried again. God, he really was beautiful, Rhys thought to himself as he let his fingers brush over Finn's soft hair. Finn increased the pressure of his sucking as he worked his mouth up and down Rhys' length and Rhys fought the urge to thrust into his mouth.

Finn had pushed the comforter completely aside when he sought out Rhys' dick so Rhys had an unobstructed view of the tight, smooth ass that was humping into the bedsheets. In fact, it was close enough to reach so Rhys took his hand from Finn's hair and stroked it over the soft skin, allowing the tip of his finger to disappear into the crease.

Finn moaned and Rhys grunted at the sensation that assaulted his dick. This time he couldn't stop himself from fucking into Finn's mouth and he felt Finn relax his jaw and throat so he could take him deeper.

Rhys used his own saliva to coat the tip of his finger before sliding it back between the globes of Finn's ass and finding his opening. Another moan from Finn as he began sucking Rhys in earnest. Finn's hand disappeared under his own hips to stroke himself as he pumped up against Rhys' finger and Rhys eventually gave him what he wanted and pushed the tip inside. It was enough to finish Finn and Rhys at nearly the same time.

Rhys watched as his come spilled from Finn's lips as he tried to swallow it all down. Rhys dragged him up for a kiss and licked the fluid from around his mouth before plunging his tongue inside. As their orgasms subsided and their bodies melted together, Finn pulled back and said with a cheeky smile, "You taste better."

~

*C*allan felt cold seep through his body as he watched Finn and Rhys laugh over something and then Rhys was spraying Finn with the water hose. He'd guessed the men had been out checking on the herd and were in the process of rinsing the sweat off their horses when they got into their little water fight. From their position, they couldn't see Callan through the barn so he had an unfettered view of their interaction and knew instantly that things had changed between the two men who'd been ready to come to blows just yesterday. They weren't being obviously overt, but a stolen touch, a sly smile, a heated stare – gestures only two people who'd been intimate with one another would share when they thought no one was watching.

He'd known it would happen at some point, but he still wasn't prepared for the keening loss that went through him. And the worst part was because he felt the loss of both men, not just one. Finn leaving him and moving on had been a foregone conclusion, but the man who gave Finn what he needed, deserved, was always some face-less individual in a world that didn't exist beyond Callan's bleak future. But to have that man be Rhys, a man he himself was feeling some invisible pull towards, was a cruel twist of fate. Karma he supposed – punishment for all the lies he'd told so he wouldn't have to spend the rest of his life watching Finn move on without him. And fucking hell if that wasn't exactly what was happening now.

"Callan?" he heard his aunt call from behind him. Her voice was high and filled with fear. He swung around and saw her hurrying down the barn aisle towards him, her hands twisting around each other.

"Are you all right?" he asked when he reached her. He heard footsteps and hooves behind him.

"It's your father – I can't find him," she cried. "He was taking a nap and I went to sit outside on the porch for just a few minutes and I must have nodded off," she said shakily.

He felt Finn's presence at his elbow and knew Rhys was likely close too.

"I woke up and went to check on him and he wasn't in bed. I can't find him anywhere!"

"It's okay, we'll find him," he said as he pulled her into his arms.

He turned to see that Finn and Rhys were already re-saddling their mounts. He turned back to Dolly and said, "Can you go back to the house and wait for him in case he gets back. Call my cell if he does. You have Finn's number too, right?" he asked.

She nodded, tears welling in her eyes. "It's so hot already, Callan. He wouldn't have thought to take any water with him," she said in a strangled voice.

Fear went through Callan and he forced himself to stay calm as he ushered Dolly back towards the house. By the time he got back to the barn, Finn and Rhys had their horses saddled and Finn was pulling Callan's black gelding from the stall.

"Finn, you take the south pasture. Rhys, can you check around the lake? He and my mother liked to go there and he doesn't remember that it's been filled in. I'll head up towards the woods on the north side of the house," he said as he tightened his horse's girth.

"Got it," Finn said. "He'll be okay, Cal," Finn reassured him and then the man was pulling him into his arms for a swift hug. Callan's anxiety overrode his common sense and he wrapped one arm around Finn's shoulders, the other around his waist and buried his face into the man's shoulder. It lasted only a few seconds, but when he looked up, he saw Rhys watching him from where he stood next to his own horse and West. The knowing, piteous look in his eyes had Callan releasing Finn and grabbing his horse's bridle and leading him from the barn without another word.

~

*C*allan held back the bile that rose in his throat as he checked his watch again. Forty-five minutes. His father had disappeared less than an hour ago, but it felt like a lifetime. The heat was sweltering and the terrain was rough and unforgiving and Callan knew that one wrong step could cost his father his life. Rattlesnakes weren't unheard of in the area and he'd even seen bear scat earlier this week near the tree line that bordered the valley the herd spent most of their time in. Guilt gnawed at Callan for the many times he'd wished he didn't have to deal with his father and the illness that was stealing him away piece by piece. The man he knew was disappearing before his very eyes, but every once in a while he got a glimpse of the proud, strong man who had taught him the value of a hard day's work when he was a little boy. The one who'd shown him how to stand up to the bigger kids that picked on him and even stick up for the ones who couldn't fight for themselves.

Tears stung Callan's eyes and he reached for his phone, ready to dial the police. He knew no one from town would help put together a search party, but he had a friend who worked for the State Patrol. It would take time to get more bodies out to help, but it was something. As he went to dial, his phone rang and a knot of fear went through him at the sight of Rhys' number.

"I got him Callan," he heard Rhys say the second he answered. "He's okay," he quickly added and Callan pulled his horse to a stop and clapped a hand over his eyes to stem the grateful tears that threatened to fall.

"Where are you?" he managed to ask

"Other side of the lake," he said. "He's pretty confused and he won't get up on the horse with me so I'm gonna find a place in the shade for us to wait near the access road. You think your aunt can get the truck down here? She's probably closest and the sooner we get him out of the heat, the better."

"Yeah, yeah, I'll call her," Callan said quickly. "Thank you, Rhys," he managed to get out. "Thank you." He ended the call before Rhys could hear the sob that had been stuck in his throat erupt. He managed to turn his horse around and head back towards the ranch. It took him a while to get his emotions under control, but he finally succeeded in getting his aunt on the phone and gave the relieved woman instructions on where to meet Rhys. He phoned Finn next, though he kept his words brief and clipped so that Finn wouldn't pick up on the distress that was coursing through him.

By the time he made it back to the ranch, his father was resting in the den and Dolly was coercing him into his second glass of ice water. Callan dropped a hand to Carter's shoulder and said, "You okay, pops?"

"Can't find the game," Carter muttered as he looked at the remote in confusion.

"Football season doesn't start for a while yet. How about some baseball?" Callan asked as he took the remote and switched the channel. His father looked okay, though his skin was slightly burned from the sun. Luckily he'd been dressed in long sleeves and khaki pants so little of his skin had been exposed.

"Have some more water," Dolly said as she handed him the glass.

"Want some beer," Carter grumbled.

"Tell you what. You finish the whole glass of water, I'll get you a beer, okay?" Dolly said. Callan felt sadness go through him because he knew that his father would forget the little white lie Dolly had told him long before he even finished the water.

He led Dolly outside the door and said, "Maybe we should take him to the ER."

Dolly shook her head. "I think that will upset him more. My friend Evelyn's on her way over. She's a nurse – retired. She said she'd check him out and then we can see if he should go in."

Callan nodded, then saw the tears brimming in Dolly's eyes.

"Callan, I'm so sorry," she whispered. "I was just so tired…"

Callan pulled her into his arms and kissed the top her head. "It's not your fault," he soothed. "You take such good care of him, Aunt Dolly. I don't know what I'd do without you," he admitted.

Dolly settled, then pulled back and wiped at her eyes, a watery laugh escaping from her trembling mouth. "I'm just full of water-works today," she said with a chuckle. "Poor Rhys probably had to go change his shirt after I got done hugging him."

Callan stiffened at the mention of Rhys and he hoped his aunt didn't notice. "I need to get my horse down to the barn and cool him off. You gonna be okay here?" he asked. She nodded, then followed him to the front door. "Call me if you need me," he said.

"I will honey," she said as she kissed his cheek. He left the house and untied his horse from the porch railing and led the sweaty animal down to the barn. As much as he owed Rhys a personal thank you, he really hoped he and Finn weren't around because he wasn't sure how much more drama he could take today. And it wasn't even fucking noon yet.

~

*R*hys moaned as Finn straddled him and languidly kissed him, his sleek tongue expertly teasing every surface before twining with his tongue. He automatically put his hands on Finn's waist and began rocking their bodies together as Finn continued his sensuous torture.

The day's long events had caught up with both of them by the time they'd made it back to the house and thrown together a quick dinner. The plan had been to finish off the sandwiches while sacked out in front of the TV watching one of the many action movies Finn had in his DVD collection, but they hadn't made it past the first gunfight before Finn was shoving their plates aside and climbing into Rhys' lap.

Callan had disappeared shortly after he'd returned from his search for his father. He'd stayed long enough to wash down his horse, then he'd gotten in the truck and just left. Finn had called him several times, but there'd been no answer. So when the head-lights flashed through the window, both he and Finn hesitated. Rhys could tell Finn wanted to say something, but was too afraid to bring it up.

"You should go check on him," Rhys said.

Finn shook his head, but the indecision lingered and Rhys couldn't help but kiss him hard. It was strange, but he knew it would bother him more if Finn was willing to dismiss Callan in favor of him. "Go. Make sure he's okay," Rhys said as he smacked Finn on the ass and lurched up, forcing the other man to his feet.

"Rhys," he said.

"Finn, if nothing else, he's your best friend. Go. I'll be here when you get back," he promised.

Finn finally nodded and hurried out of the house. Rhys went to his room and stripped off his sweat stained clothes and climbed into the shower. It had been a relief to find Callan's father, but the man's confusion and surly attitude had made it difficult to deal with him. Aunt Dolly had been a piece of work too, but in a really good way. After she'd finished crying all over him and fussing over her brother, she'd taken charge of Carter and had him packed away in the truck within a few minutes. Since he'd had to walk his horse back, she'd driven ahead so she could get her brother into the safety of the air conditioned house, but she'd made him promise to stop by the house for a real talk soon. It was yet another connection he probably shouldn't be making, but he couldn't help but want to ask her what Callan was like as a kid.

He'd never seen the man so close to falling apart as he was when Finn had comforted him before they separated on their searches today. Between Callan's reaction to the news that his father was missing and the information he'd managed to glean from the confused, older man, Rhys was starting to understand why Callan had been hiding who he was for so long.

Rhys stepped out of the shower and pulled on a pair of running pants. He'd just tugged on a T-shirt when Finn came into his room, the worry clear on his face.

"He wouldn't talk to me," he said quietly as he sat on Rhys' bed. "He wouldn't even open the door."

"He'll be okay Finn. It was a lot for him to deal with today."

Finn nodded, though he didn't look like he really believed what he was silently agreeing to. Rhys leaned down and kissed Finn, then pulled him to his feet. "Go get cleaned up. You'll feel better," he urged. Finn reached up to stroke his fingers over Rhys' mouth, his eyes heavy with those damn emotions Rhys needed to stop reading too much into.

Finn went across the hall and to his own bathroom. As soon as Rhys heard the water come on, he grabbed the tools he'd need and left the house. Callan's house sat only a hundred feet away and was modeled exactly like Finn's. It took Rhys a little longer to pick the lock on the front door since it was both pitch black inside and outside, but he was in the house within a few minutes.

The front part of the house was empty so Rhys made his way to the bedrooms, worry gnawing at him. He entered the bigger of the two bedrooms and came to a stop when he saw Callan sitting on the edge of the bed, a bottle in his hand. The bathroom light was on, casting enough reach into the bedroom to show that the bottle was still mostly full.

"Isn't breaking and entering a parole violation?" Callan said with a grunt as he took a long draw from the bottle.

Rhys ignored the jab and leaned against the doorframe. "Finn's worried about you."

"He'll get over it. Like you keep telling me, he's a big boy." Callan started to take another drink, but Rhys reached him before the bottle touched his lips. He snatched the bottle and carried it into the bathroom. Nearly half of it was already down the drain by the time Callan grabbed him and shoved him against the sink. "Fuck off, Rhys," he said with a snarl as he tried to take the bottle back.

Rhys dropped the bottle into the sink and brought his arm down on Callan's to loosen his hold, then twisted it behind him and shoved him away. "So this is how's it's going to be, huh, Callan? You'd rather drown your lies in booze instead of live your life?"

"Go to hell," Callan responded, his voice dropping off.

"I get it," Rhys said as he emptied the rest of the bottle and dropped it into the trash bin next to the sink. "Believe me, I fucking get it." He leaned back against the sink. "I know why your father wandered off today."

He saw Callan stiffen, but the stubborn man remained mute.

"He kept telling me he had to go meet you at the bus stop because he was going to take you fishing after you got done with school. Said it was your favorite thing."

Callan leaned his head back against the wall and closed his eyes, the fight going out of him. "What else did he say?"

Rhys chuckled slightly. "Well, he was kind of all over the place but there was mention of no one sitting a horse better than you, straight A's on your report card all through high school and how you and he were gonna run the ranch side by side when you grew up." Rhys closed the distance between himself and the other man and clasped his hand over Callan's cheek, forcing him to meet his gaze. "You lost him before you got a chance to see if he would accept you for who you really are, didn't you? And now you're stuck being the son he remembers instead of the son you would have been."

Callan's hand reached up and closed around Rhys' wrist. "He wouldn't have accepted me," he said softly. "I had so many chances to tell him when I was younger and I didn't and then it was too late. I was a fucking coward."

"You don't owe him your future, Callan."

"So I should just walk away from him? Away from the man who gave me life, who protected me? Am I supposed to leave him when he needs me most?" Callan pulled Rhys' hand away from his cheek. "Or am I supposed to ask Finn – or any other man for that matter – to stay in a place where we could never really be together?" Callan straightened and tried to move past Rhys to leave the bathroom.

"Things can change if you fight! This town can change! Fight for what you want, damn it!" Rhys said as he slammed Callan back against the wall.

"At what cost, Rhys? You've been here a week. You saw one cut fence and one hurt calf. Tell me again how I should fight when half your herd is lying dead or dying around you. When you have to wonder if that sip of water you just took from the well will kill you like it did them. When you're always looking over your shoulder for the next attack and knowing that no one will be there to help you when it comes."

Callan got right up in Rhys' face. "You tell me how to fight when you watch the man you love die a little more each day because he's surrounded by people who hate him because he doesn't want to play by their rules. You tell me how to fight when you're lying awake night after night praying that he's not the one those cowards go after next instead of just your fences or your cattle or your checkbook!"

"Cal?"

Rhys heard Callan's sharp intake of breath as the quiet, confused voice broke through. They both turned at the same time to see Finn standing just outside the bathroom door and Rhys knew by the horror and shock on his face that the young man had heard Callan's declaration of love.

84

CHAPTER 11

*C*allan's entire world imploded at the sound of Finn's broken voice and he leaned back against the wall for support.

"Finn," he heard Rhys say as he left the bathroom and reached for the younger man.

"Don't touch me. Don't you fucking touch me!" Finn shouted as he wrapped his arms around himself. He stepped around Rhys and stopped in the doorway of the bathroom.

"How long, Callan?" Callan raised his eyes to Finn's and saw the fury burning there, as well as the devastation.

Callan again, not Cal.

"How long?" Finn yelled.

"What Finn?" Callan finally said tiredly. "How long have I known I was gay or how long have I been in love with you?"

Finn stepped back as if he'd been physically punched.

"Finn," Rhys tried again, but Finn whirled on him. "You knew?" Rhys nodded.

"I asked him not to tell you," Callan said.

"Shut the fuck up, Callan!" he screamed, then turned his attention back to Rhys. "Last night?" he asked, his voice dropping to a near whisper as agony tore through him. "Is that why you didn't want to fuck me last night?"

Callan watched as Rhys shifted uneasily.

"Jesus, were you," Finn started to say but seemed to get hung up on the next words. "Were you saving me for him?" Tears flowed down Finn's face as he laughed hysterically, the sound ripping like a knife through Callan. "Oh my God," Finn cried.

Rhys grabbed Finn who instantly tried to pull away from him. "What happened between us last night was everything I said it was, Finn!"

"Get your fucking hands off me!"

"Finn, stop it!" Callan finally said.

Finn ripped free of Rhys and spun around. He looked like was going to start raging again, but then all the fight went out of him. "You've ruined me," he said so quietly that Callan struggled to hear him. Finn shook his head, almost as if in wonder. Tears streamed down his face. "You've ruined me, Cal," he repeated, then turned and brushed past Rhys.

Callan felt his insides rip open as he watched Finn leave him forever. He looked up at Rhys, but the other man wasn't moving. Callan bent over as nausea swept through him. This had always been the plan – to let Finn go. But now that it was happening, he couldn't remember any of the reasons he was supposed to let it. All he could think of was that Finn wouldn't be there with his sunny smile in the morning as he fed the horses or got West ready so they could ride out and check the fences together. He wouldn't be there to laugh that loud, all-in laugh or crack his weird jokes that only made sense to him. There'd be no more silly grins or serious conversations or shared victories. Losing Finn meant losing himself, losing that one last part of him that was honest and true.

Callan was moving before he could talk himself out of it and was running by the time he got to the bedroom door. Finn was in the process of opening the front door when Callan slammed into him from behind and forced the door shut.

"Please don't," he whispered against the back of Finn's neck as he wrapped his arm around the other man's waist.

Finn closed his hand over the one Callan had on his abdomen and tried to pry it off. "No!" he said in a husky voice. He tried to open the door, but Callan was stronger and it didn't budge.

Callan twisted Finn around so that they were facing and forced him to look up. "Please Finn, I'm begging you," he whispered as he leaned down and brushed his mouth over Finn's trembling lips. They were as soft and sweet as he dreamed they would be, though he'd always imagined Finn's shaking would be from lust, not fury. A sob escaped Finn as Callan kissed him lightly again, then pulled back.

"Tell him everything, Callan," Rhys said from behind him.

Callan felt Finn still beneath his touch and he forced himself to take a deep breath. He could do this. He needed to do this.

"I knew I preferred men in high school, but I didn't do anything about it until I was away at college." Callan felt a surge of relief go through him as Finn relaxed slightly in his hold, indicating that he was at least going to listen. He cast a glance over his shoulder and saw that Rhys was standing on the other side of the entryway near the hallway that led to the bedrooms. There was enough light from the bedroom to see Rhys' expression as he gave Callan a supportive nod. He felt a surge of strength go through him and he turned back to Finn and closed his hands around the other man's upper arms, his thumbs rubbing small circles into Finn's warm skin. He hadn't noticed until now that Finn was shirtless and wore only a set of thin pants as pajama bottoms.

"I kept trying to figure out how to tell my father, but I'd seen and heard how he talked about gay people since the time I was a little kid and I knew in my gut that he wouldn't accept me. So I hid it. I dated women, even managed to sleep with some. I was twenty-one when I finally fucked a guy for the first time and after that I couldn't get enough. So I spent my days getting good grades and flirting with pretty girls and my nights fucking random men at a gay club outside of town. Then I went home on weekends and told my dad about all the women I was dating."

Callan felt a knot of anxiety go through him and then his breathing started to go shallow. *Jesus, not now*. Before his vision started to dim, he saw Finn looking at him with concern and if he hadn't been struggling to breathe, it would have given him some measure of hope that maybe he could still fix this.

"Callan," he heard someone call him and then a broad palm was stroking over his back. "Callan, just focus on your breathing. In and out, real slow." *Rhys*.

Callan closed his eyes and focused on Rhys' voice as he counted off the breaths and finally after several long, painful seconds, he felt his lungs start to ease and the pressure in his chest began to fade.

"Cal?"

Callan wanted to cry at hearing Finn call him by his nickname. His eyes focused and he realized he'd ended up on his knees on the floor. Finn was still in front of him, though he too had dropped down onto the floor. Rhys was at his back, still rubbing circles in his back with his hand. God, he wished it was over and this was exactly where he could spend the rest of his life – between the man who'd brought light into his dark world and the man he knew would always be there to catch him if he fell. He reached out a hand to Finn's cheek and brushed it briefly before dropping it.

"I kept going to the club, but I was never very selective about who I was with. I was too afraid to let any of them fuck me so I only went after the ones who were willing to bottom. One night I picked the wrong guy. We went to the alley behind the club. His friends were waiting there…" Callan started to feel his breath catch so he closed his eyes and reached his hand behind his back and felt Rhys grab it and squeeze hard.

Finn's fingers on his face had him opening up his eyes. "Tell me," he said gently.

Callan nodded, then said, "There were three of them. They hit and kicked me until I couldn't fight anymore and then they took turns. They held my wrists-" he managed to say before a sob overtook him.

"It's okay, Cal, you don't have to say anymore," Finn said as he reached up and placed a kiss on Callan's forehead.

"I need to finish it," Cal said.

Finn nodded, then took Cal's free hand between his own.

"I went to the ER and they called the cops. I told them what happened. They said they could try to find the guys, but that then everyone would know the truth about why I was there to begin with. They told me that I had put myself at risk by going to the club in the first place and if they brought charges against the men, I'd have to testify. They said they needed to call my dad to come get me," Callan explained. "I left before they did the rape kit and I told my father I'd been mugged. I haven't been with anyone since. I kissed Rhys, but panicked when he touched me," Callan finished.

Finn was quiet for a long time before he finally said, "I'm so sorry that happened to you, Cal. But I don't understand why you lied to me." He dropped his eyes. "Especially after you must've known how I felt about you."

Callan ran his fingers through Finn's hair. "I was a coward, Finn. At first I thought you just had a crush on me – you were so young. I kept trying to keep that image of you being a kid in my head even after I started wanting you because it made my choice to live a lie seem easier."

"All these years I've trusted you. Without question," Finn said sadly. "I stayed in this town, let those people shit all over me because we were friends and I didn't want to lose that. I tried to walk away so many times, but you wouldn't let me go."

"I was selfish. I thought I could somehow have you and still keep the promises I made," Callan sighed. "I'm so sorry, Finn." He knew they were reaching a point where Finn would walk away from him again so he leaned down and kissed him. "I wish I could be the man you deserve."

One last kiss. He needed one more. Callan pulled Finn up to meet him as he licked over his lips and whispered, "One taste, Finn. Please, I just need one taste."

Finn whimpered, then opened his mouth and let Callan in. Desire sparked through him at the taste of Finn and he used his tongue to explore every surface of Finn's soft mouth before he stroked his tongue over Finn's. It was a thousand times better then he'd ever imagined. He angled his head so he could get deeper inside that mouth and then his hands were pulling Finn up against his body. Tight, smooth skin greeted his touch and muscles rippled beneath his palms as he gripped Finn's upper back.

Callan let his lips trail down Finn's neck, then he shifted them both so that they were facing Rhys who had remained on his knees behind him. The other man was watching them with sad acceptance, then actually made a move to get up and Callan instantly knew what he was thinking. He grabbed Rhys' hand and pulled him back down, then wrapped his hand around Rhys' neck and pulled him in for a long, deep kiss. Their tongues clashed as the kiss turned needy and then they were both turning their attention on Finn who'd been watching them in awe. Callan kissed Finn's mouth as Rhys began a slow perusal of the skin over Finn's collarbone.

Callan managed to pull back from Finn long enough to whisper, "One night Finn. Give me one night. I have no right to ask, but I need you. I need both of you," he said, his eyes moving from Finn to Rhys.

Long seconds passed as each man studied him in turn, then Finn was kissing him again, his soft "yes" hard to hear over the ringing in his ears. As he leaned back to watch Finn kiss Rhys, Callan knew that the memory of what would happen next would have to last him a lifetime because come morning, he'd be alone again.

～

Finn shook as Cal pulled him to his feet and he wasn't sure if it was nerves, need, or shock. Probably all three, he mused as Cal kissed him again. His entire life had irrevocably changed in the last five minutes and he was likely about to make things worse. He knew that if he told Cal no, everything would end and Cal would let him go this time, no argument. Betrayal was burning inside him like acid, but the need to be with Cal and Rhys was just a little bit greater. He wasn't even at a point where he could safely process Cal's admission of love, so he focused on the moment and nothing else.

Between Cal and Rhys taking turns kissing him, Finn wasn't sure how he'd make it to the second act because his body was on the verge of exploding. And if that wasn't enough, watching the two men drown in each other had him reaching for his cock. He would have expected to feel jealousy, but he just wanted more. More of all of it.

Cal turned back to him and suddenly grabbed the backs of his thighs and lifted him. He automatically wrapped around Cal, then opened his mouth when Cal began kissing him again. As Cal began walking towards the bedroom, Finn's eyes latched on to Rhys who was right behind them, stripping off his T-shirt. God, was this really happening?

Finn felt himself falling backwards and his back bounced on the mattress. Cal was on him instantly, the sweet, slow kisses giving way to hard, needy drags. Light flooded the room and then the mattress dipped as Rhys settled next to them and Cal rolled them so he and Finn were facing. Firm lips coasted over his back and shoulders, then latched on to his neck as an arm snaked around his waist. Both men finally gave him a moment to catch his breath as hands and mouths worked their way down his body. Then he was flat on his back again as Cal worked his pajama bottoms off and Rhys sucked one of his nipples into his mouth.

Finn hissed at the pleasure that surged through him, then arched violently as Cal sucked the tip of his cock into his mouth. Finn dug his fingers into Rhys' back as the man continued to suck and kiss his way down towards his abdomen. A hot tongue dipped into his belly button, then went lower. As Cal worked him in deeper, Finn felt Rhys shift and then suddenly Cal's mouth was releasing him. Finn leaned up on his elbows to beg him not to stop, then lost the ability to speak when he saw Cal and Rhys kissing, their mouths just inches from his aching dick. He didn't want to do anything to stop it, so he hung there and enjoyed the sight of the two men battling over control of the kiss. Rhys finally won and Finn knew exactly the pleasure Cal would be experiencing as that talented tongue fucked in and out of his mouth.

The show only lasted for a minute before two sets of eyes latched onto his. Before he could even consider what might happen next, two tongues curled around his pulsing length. With one man on each side of him and mouths working in tandem, Finn knew he was a goner and he dropped back down on the bed and closed his eyes as the tingle in his spine signaled the end. Someone's mouth closed over his cock – he wasn't sure whose – and he felt a tongue dip back into his mouth. He didn't need to open his eyes to know it was Rhys who claimed his mouth because his and Cal's unique flavors would be burned into his mind forever.

"I'm gonna come," he managed to say as his balls drew up almost painfully.

"Watch him, baby," Rhys whispered as he shifted Finn's shoulders up and dragged his upper body against him so Finn could see what Cal was doing to him. "Watch him drink down every drop," he said against Finn's ear as he licked the sensitive skin there.

Cal dragged up and down his length slowly, twisting his tongue around the shaft on each stroke. Blunt fingers curled around his balls and massaged them as Cal pulled off long enough to let some saliva dribble down onto Finn's supersensitive cock. Finn was so close, but he needed that final push.

"Please, Cal," he said hoarsely and shuddered when those nearly gray eyes collided with his. Cal watched him intently for a moment and Finn reached out to clutch Rhys' hand, needing something to ground him. Then Cal was back on him and sucking hard, his head bobbing up and down. And he never took his eyes off of Finn. Two more hard tugs, then Cal went all the way down to the root and swallowed.

Finn cried out as he came and he forced his eyes to stay open as he watched his body thrust deeper into Cal's mouth. Spurt after endless spurt shot out of his body, but Cal never lost a drop and didn't release him even after Finn collapsed against Rhys' chest, the orgasm draining him. Cal's tongue continued to gently suck him, then licked him clean while Rhys kissed him. Then Cal's mouth was on his again, but Finn couldn't find the strength to do anything but lay there and let Cal love him. And then his men were kissing each other once again and a spark of need began to coil in Finn as he felt Cal's erection pressed up against his hips as Cal straddled him.

He saw Cal's hand close over Rhys' cock as Rhys leaned in further so their bodies were nearly aligned from the waist up. Finn reached his own hand down and curled it around Cal's length and watched in satisfaction as Cal's eyes keyed in on his.

~

Callan closed his eyes as Rhys' lips closed over the skin on his neck and Finn's hand began stroking him slowly. The taste of Finn still lingered in his mouth and he wished he had the stamina to combine it with Rhys' flavor. But he knew that if he didn't get inside Finn soon, he wouldn't last. And this night had to last him a fucking lifetime. Callan reached out with his free hand to pull Rhys in for another drugging kiss as he continued to play with the man's cock. He felt Finn stiffen further beneath him, a clear sign that the sight of him and Rhys kissing turned Finn on.

Callan buried his hand in Rhys' hair and forced Rhys to release him. His eyes met the other man's and he said, "I want you inside me," then looked down at Finn. "I want you inside me while I'm inside him." Finn's eyes widened and his lips parted. The younger man's erection was back in full force.

"Callan," Rhys began. "You don't have to-"

He kissed Rhys hard before releasing him again. "I trust you. Both of you," he said firmly, his eyes dropping down to Finn briefly. "Rhys, I want this so bad,' he said in a strangled voice. And it was true. He'd waited a lifetime for this moment with Finn, but he'd give it up in a second if it didn't include Rhys. Callan had no idea how the other man had become so important to him so quickly, but he wasn't going to question it – not tonight anyway. He was giving himself this one night to have the life he wanted. He kissed Rhys again, slowly this time, and sighed when he felt the acquiescence go through the other man.

"Finn, nightstand," he managed to say between Rhys' bone melting kisses. A condom was pressed into his hand and he forced himself to release Rhys' lips long enough to work the latex down the man's erection. Nerves went through him as he realized how thick Rhys really was and a twinge of panic skittered down his spine. But then Rhys' hands were stroking his chest and curling around his back. The man's instinct for knowing when Callan needed his touch was uncanny and that reminder of how much he really did trust Rhys had him searching out the bottle of lube Finn had placed by his knee.

Callan turned his attention back on Finn and leaned down and trailed his fingers over the man's lips. "Are you sure about this?" he asked, hoping to God Finn hadn't changed his mind.

Finn nodded, then pulled Callan down for a kiss. He felt Rhys shift behind him and big hands caressed down his sides and over his hips. Callan released Finn's mouth, then sat up and pulled Finn further down the bed and bent his legs back and shifted his ass higher, exposing the pretty hole waiting for him. He took the bottle of lube Rhys handed him and poured some on his fingers, then skimmed them over the fluttering opening. Finn closed his eyes at the contact, then tensed up when Callan pushed the tip of his finger inside him. Callan pulled back a little before pushing back in until his second knuckle disappeared into the hot body twitching beneath him. One more drag and his finger was in as far as it could go.

"So tight," he muttered as he pulled his finger out, then pushed it and another finger all the way in. Finn moaned and spread himself wider. Callan sensed Rhys watching him, then felt the other man's front press into his back as his arms came around Callan and grabbed Finn's legs to hold him open. Callan could feel Rhys' erection against his own ass and the excitement of knowing he would soon be connected to these two men in a way no one could ever take from him had his fingers trembling as they twisted and scissored inside of Finn. On his next pass, he searched out the spongy spot inside of Finn that he knew would have him seeing stars and was rewarded with a loud shout.

"Fuck! Jesus, what is that?" Finn cried in pleasure as Callan nailed him again.

"Your sweet spot, baby," Rhys managed to say, his voice husky with need.

"Oh God, Cal, stop or I'm going to come," Finn said as he reached above his head to grab the headboard.

Callan eased off his prostate and added a third finger. Finn's whole body was drawn tight. "You okay?" Callan whispered as he held his fingers still. Finn looked up at him, his eyes bright with passion. He managed a nod, but couldn't get any words out. Callan carefully pulled his fingers free, then lined up his cock and began to breach Finn's body. Whimpers left Finn's mouth as Callan gave him shallow strokes, dipping in a little further inside of the tight channel on each pass. Callan's own body was on fire and sweat dripped mercilessly down his brow as he tried to maintain control.

"He's so tight, Rhys," Callan got out as his cock finally slid all the way in. "Jesus," he said as Finn's muscles clamped down on him. He saw Finn reach out his hand and Callan quickly grabbed and held it, knowing the younger man was drowning in the overwhelming emotion. Callan held him as he pulled out and pushed back in slowly, still letting Finn's body adjust to the invasion.

Rhys released Finn's legs and his hand ran down Callan's spine. "Talk to me, Callan. Tell me you still want this," Rhys said as he skimmed his lips along Callan's upper back.

Callan reached around and grabbed Rhys left hand with his and pulled it around to his chest. He intertwined their fingers and said, "I want this." He turned Rhys' hand over and placed a kiss on the palm, then released him. Rhys' lips drifted over the back of his neck once more, then Callan felt himself being pushed gently down onto Finn, his cock pressing deeper into the other man.

Finn's arms closed around him as they kissed. Cold lube dripped onto his hole and then Rhys' fingers were there, probing him. The pressure of one finger entering him burned and a flash of fear went through him, but then Finn was pulling him down and plundering his mouth, his slick tongue teasing him. He could feel Finn's cock pressed between their bodies, the pre-come leaking against his abdomen. The words telling Rhys to hurry never made it past his lips because another finger slid into him, long and deep and within seconds a third joined it. He moaned when Rhys massaged his prostate, then felt Finn smile against his lips as he realized Callan was experiencing the same insurmountable pleasure he'd been tortured with only moments earlier.

Rhys' fingers slid out of him and Callan tensed as he felt the blunt head of Rhys' cock begin to stretch him. Callan wrapped himself around Finn and moaned as Rhys slid all the way inside, his body pushing Callan further into Finn. The dual pressure was playing havoc with Callan's mind and he wanted to cry out at the knot that unfurled inside him as it hit him that this was exactly where he was supposed to be.

"Cal," Finn whispered. Callan opened his eyes and looked down at Finn who was watching him with concern. It took him a moment to realize that tears were sliding down his own cheeks and he managed a watery laugh as he kissed Finn briefly.

"I'm okay," Callan said softly.

Rhys began to increase his pace and Callan felt fingers press into his hips as Rhys' cock drilled in and out of him. Finn gripped his upper arms as Callan's own cock thrust in and out as Callan began shifting his hips back to meet Rhys' strokes. The combined friction in his ass and around his cock had him grinding hard against each man and he leaned up to brace his arms on either side of Finn as he pummeled in and out of the man's pulsing body. Rhys matched the rhythm and within minutes Callan's body began to shake from the exertion. Electricity danced along his spine and sparks lit up under his skin. Knowing he was close, he reached down and wrapped his hand around Finn's cock and stroked him mercilessly. Finn cried out at the contact and lifted his ass higher so Callan could get even deeper.

He angled his hips so that he could hit Finn's prostate and he shouted in pleasure when Rhys did the same to him. Skin slapped against skin as their slick bodies worked in tandem and then Finn flew over, his release shooting between them as his rectum clamped down on Callan's cock. He felt Rhys' cock thicken and pulse inside him, then a heavy hand clamped down on his shoulder as Rhys shot into him. Callan's own body gave up the fight and he thrust one last time into Finn and held there as the orgasm ripped through his nerve endings, flaying him alive with exquisite relief. Rhys continued pumping into him as Callan dropped onto Finn and then he felt Rhys' body mold over his as he humped into him a few more times as his own release eased.

Finn's lips claimed his, then Rhys was pulling his head around for a taste and then Callan was gone, floating into an abyss of pleasure and peace that he'd craved his whole life. Just before his eyes closed, he managed one last look at Finn and knew in that moment it would be his last because Finn would be gone by morning.

CHAPTER 12

*C*allan let the hot water sluice over his back as he closed his eyes and tried to push back the overwhelming sadness that had set in the instant he woke up alone in his bed. He hadn't felt either Finn or Rhys leave him, testament to how worn out he'd been by the events of the evening before, and he'd expected they'd leave before he awoke, but the reality of it still hurt. It had felt good to be held throughout the night and the few times he'd awoken, he'd found himself surrounded in heat and warmth as Rhys wrapped around him from behind and Finn cuddled up along his front.

Callan forced himself to turn off the water and get dried off. Today would be like any other day. Work, food, sleep. He'd gotten what he wanted – the night he'd dreamed of with Finn and Rhys and the assurance that Finn would have a shot at the future he craved. The younger man would settle down with someone kind and loyal and generous and Rhys would head back to the big city and rebuild the life he'd had before prison. And Callan would ride fences and build out his herd and live up to the standards that had been set for him. Everything was as it should be.

It was complete bullshit and not even he was a good enough liar to fool himself. Callan pulled on his clothes and walked out of the bedroom, then slowed as he heard his aunt's voice.

"Honey, he used to sneak out to the barn every night and sleep with his horse. Nearly gave his mama a heart attack the first time he did it," she said with a hearty laugh. Callan turned the corner and came to a halt when he saw his aunt sitting across the small kitchen table from Rhys, full cups of coffee in front of each of them.

Emerald eyes lifted to meet his as Rhys took a drink and those amazing lips spared him a quick grin before he returned his attention back to Dolly. The walls Callan had spent the last hour rebuilding came crashing down around him at the sight of Rhys and he actually had to put a hand against the wall to keep himself upright.

Dolly finally noticed his presence and turned in her chair, a huge smile splitting her lips. "Morning darling," she said as she turned back to the table and grabbed an empty mug sitting in the middle and started filling it with coffee for him.

"You're up early, Aunt Dolly," Callan mused as he stepped into the kitchen.

"I made some cookies for you boys last night and I wanted to drop them off before your father wakes up," she said, glancing at her watch. "And then Rhys and I got to talking…"

Callan saw Rhys subtly stiffen and he quickly said, "I was telling Dolly how I came over early this morning to get my list of chores and you asked me to get some coffee started while you were finishing up," he said lamely. Callan's heart shifted at Rhys' effort to protect him with a bogus story. Yesterday Rhys had been urging him to fight, to stand up for himself and Finn, yet here he was trying to come up with some crappy lie to protect him from the very thing Callan had spent his whole life running from.

"Rhys didn't stop by, Aunt Dolly. He spent the night here," Callan said, then dropped a hand onto Rhys' shoulder to make it completely clear to his aunt what he was saying. Rhys stiffened beneath his touch and both men fell silent as it took Dolly a few, long moments to process what he was saying. Since he was all in anyway, Callan said, "Finn too."

Dolly studied him, then looked at Rhys. Callan felt something break inside as he wondered what it would be like to lose the woman who'd been like a mother to him since his own had passed so long ago.

"Well, where is he?"

Callan looked down at Rhys in confusion, then back at Dolly. "Who?"

"Finn, of course," she responded matter of factly.

Callan felt like he was underwater and actually couldn't manage to form any words.

"He had some stuff to do this morning," Rhys interjected.

Dolly stood and pulled Callan down to plant a kiss on his cheek. "Well, I hope I didn't interrupt anything this morning," she said with a hearty chuckle as she brushed past Callan and wrapped her arms around Rhys' neck. "And you, you go make my boy some breakfast – Lord knows he can't cook to save his own life," she snorted.

"Yes ma'am," Rhys said and he actually got up and went to the refrigerator and started pulling out food.

Callan was completely shell-shocked and Dolly actually took his mug from him so he wouldn't spill coffee all over himself.

"I'll see you later, darling," she said as she patted his arm.

"Wait, that's it?" he managed to say.

"What's it?" she asked innocently. He motioned between himself and Rhys who was grinning like an idiot. "Callan, for God's sake, do you think I just walked out of a corn patch somewhere? This town might be ass backwards, but I lived in San Francisco in the seventies. The nice young man who lived in the apartment below mine used to borrow my dresses and taught me how to put on my makeup," Dolly said with exasperation.

"I don't think Callan will want to borrow your dresses, Dolly," Rhys said from behind him. Dolly laughed heartily.

"I'll make you boys some lasagna for dinner. How does that sound?" she said as she went to the door.

"Sounds good," Callan said with a smile. He turned to see Rhys watching him with a soft smile, then the man focused his attention on what he was cooking.

What the hell had just happened?

~

*R*hys was in the middle of cracking an egg when hands closed on his waist and spun him around. Callan's mouth fastened on his and then his tongue was stroking deep into Rhys' mouth. Callan pushed him up against the refrigerator and Rhys barely managed to get the burner on the stove turned off before Callan was working his shirt off. Callan's palms dragged down Rhys' chest and then curled around his back and settled on his ass.

Having Callan initiate an encounter with him was the last thing Rhys had expected, but he wasn't about to argue the point. He'd struggled with how he was going to get his perspective back after the red hot night he'd spent with the other two men, especially after waking up to find Finn gone. Callan had looked so worn out that Rhys had let him sleep and had left the house to change clothes. But the idea of Callan waking up alone after everything that had happened seemed wrong so he'd made his way back to the other man's house.

He'd just finished brewing the coffee when there'd been a knock on the door and his only thought had been that it would be Finn and it didn't occur to him not to answer it. Then he'd seen Dolly standing there, clearly taken aback by his presence and the need to keep Callan's secret had reared up and the lie fell easily from his lips. A nice conversation with Dolly about Callan's antics as a youngster had followed, then Callan was there and blurting out that he'd spent the night not just with one man, but two.

"I want you," Callan said against his lips and then he was kissing Rhys' neck as fingers began working the button and zipper on his jeans.

Rhys desperately wanted to ask Callan if he was enough for him – if they could have something without Finn being there, but his insecurity had him nodding his head instead. A hand disappeared inside his pants and then he was engulfed in a tight grip as Callan's mouth returned to his. He thrust into Callan's hold, then watched hungrily as

Callan used his free hand to shove the pants down, then dropped to his knees. Wet heat surrounded him as Callan sucked him deep. Rhys grabbed his hair and rammed further down his throat and moaned as Callan relaxed his jaw and let him in as far as he could go. Fingers bit into his ass as Rhys fucked into Callan's mouth over and over.

"Fuck," Rhys moaned as he slowed his strokes and just enjoyed the sight of his dick sliding seamlessly in and out of Callan's willing mouth. Callan let him have a few more seconds of the agonizing pleasure, then the man reared up, grabbed Rhys and shoved him face down on the kitchen table. Rhys pushed the few dishes that had been there aside, then steeled himself as Callan leaned over him, his front molding to Rhys' back. Hard muscle glided over hard muscle and then that tongue was sliding down his spine. Before he could process what was happening, Callan had split him open and his mouth closed over Rhys' hole and sucked.

Rhys clenched the sides of the table and dropped his forehead to the cold wood as Callan licked and bit at him. He'd never had this done to him before and hadn't even considered it with previous partners. But he knew the second he got the chance, he'd reciprocate with Callan. And Finn. A brief pang of loss went through him at the thought of the young man, but then Callan was pressing his tongue inside of him and everything but sensation left him.

"Callan, please," he begged as his body began to burn and twitch. His cock ached, but there was no way he could reach it from his position.

"What do you want, Rhys?" Callan whispered against his hole, the soft puff of breath caressing the tortured flesh.

"I want you to fuck me," Rhys moaned as he tried to press back against Callan's face.

Callan rose back to his feet, then leaned over Rhys and forced his head back for a bone melting kiss. He released Rhys and for a panic filled moment, Rhys thought he was stopping because Callan stepped away from him. But then Callan was back and he felt something slick brush over his hole. Vegetable oil. He'd had it out so he could use it to make the eggs.

Callan pressed a soaking finger inside of Rhys, working the oil in deep. He got only a few seconds before another finger joined the first.

"I can't wait," Callan said as he pulled his fingers out. Rhys didn't even get a chance to tell him it was okay before Callan's thick cock began pushing into him. The pressure and burn were intense, but Rhys wanted more and he braced himself on his elbows so he could counter Callan's efforts to ease inside him.

"Oh God," Callan moaned as he pulled out and slid back in. "It's so good, Rhys," he said as he began long, smooth glides in and out of Rhys. Fingers curled over Rhys' shoulders and held him as Callan quickened his pace.

Suddenly Callan came to a grinding halt and Rhys nearly shouted at him not to stop.

"Shit, I forgot the condom," he said, then pulled all the way out. "Rhys, I'm so sorry," he said.

"Callan, don't stop, please! I've been tested. I'm negative, I swear," Rhys heard himself say and he hardly recognized the begging tone that fell from his lips. It would only take a minute for Callan to search out a condom, but Rhys wanted nothing between them.

"I need all of you." Rhys whispered his final plea as he dropped his forehead to the table, the need and vulnerability making him feel exposed like a raw nerve.

Callan was quiet for so long that Rhys actually started to move. But then a hard hand was pushing him back down and Callan slammed into him, his control clearly gone. There was no latex separating them so Rhys felt every brush against his inner walls. Each time Callan pounded into him the table lurched forward until it finally hit the wall and stopped, giving Callan the leverage he needed to power into Rhys over and over.

Rhys felt his shoulders being pressed down as Callan all but climbed on top of him as he fucked him harder and harder. A shift in the angle of Callan's hips had him brushing Rhys' prostate and everything went light and dark at the same time. Rhys heard himself telling Callan that he needed it harder, though the voice didn't sound like his own. His cock was pinned painfully against the table, but Rhys didn't care because Callan's movements were giving him enough friction to have his balls drawing up tight. Tension built and built inside of Rhys until it suddenly snapped like a rubber band and he was screaming as his come pooled beneath him, slick and hot. Callan shouted in his ear as he thrust one last time and then warm liquid flooded Rhys' insides and Callan bit down on the back of his neck as shudders racked his body.

Several minutes passed as they both tried to catch their breath and Callan's cock softened inside him and the other man pulled free of him. Rhys could only lay there as he felt the come seep out his body and he wondered if Callan was enjoying the sight or sickened by it. He felt fingers suddenly enter him and then Callan was leaning over him and whispering, "I wish I had a plug so you could feel me inside of you for the rest of the day."

Rhys shuddered at the dirty talk and lifted his head for the kiss he knew Callan would give him. The fingers slid out of him and Callan pulled his boneless body to his feet. Rhys didn't protest when Callan dragged him into the shower and cleaned him from head to toe and he had nothing to say when Callan sat him back down at the table, fully dressed and finished making breakfast. The topic that Callan had smoothly managed to sidestep with mind-blowing sex was back.

"He's gone," Rhys finally said with a sigh.

∼

"Yep, you've got it," Dane said to Finn as Finn pressed the last tab in place. He lifted Emma up and smiled when the diaper didn't fall off. Finn dropped down into one of the kitchen chairs and cuddled the quiet, gurgling baby against his chest. Her clear eyes looked up at him with wonder and as soon as he stuck one of his fingers out, she grabbed it.

"Here," Dane said as he handed him a bottle. Emma began bouncing in his arms at the sight of her milk and instantly opened her mouth as Finn pressed it against her tiny lips. Dane slid a stack of pancakes in front of Finn, then sat next to him.

"Here, I can take her," Dane offered.

Finn actually kept the baby from his reach, then felt a flush of embarrassment light up his cheeks as he realized what he'd done. "No, I don't mind," he stammered.

Dane smiled in understanding and began working on his own breakfast.

"Thanks for letting me barge in on you guys so early," Finn said as he forked some food into his mouth with one hand while he used his cheek to hold the bottle in place.

"Eight o'clock for us isn't early," Dane said with a chuckle. The man took a few more bites, then finally did what Finn had been expecting and said, "You want to tell me what happened?"

He didn't. He really didn't. It had been early when he'd woken up in Cal's arms. They'd been facing each other and Finn had allowed himself a few precious moments to study the man while he peacefully slept. He'd looked so much younger and relaxed than Finn had ever seen him and the love he had for Cal had exploded to new heights as he remembered how it felt to have Cal rocking inside his body, his penetrating gaze holding back none of his emotions. If he'd had any doubt about Cal telling the truth when he told Rhys he loved Finn, it had died the instant Cal had entered him. But the betrayal had been a cold bedfellow to wake up with and no amount of the warmth that radiated from Cal's body could take that way. And he hadn't even started to factor in Rhys.

His anger towards Cal had been amplified at knowing Rhys had lied to him as well. It was something he hadn't expected since Rhys had been open and up front from day one. The rational side knew that Rhys had been trying to protect Cal, but it didn't take the sting away. And knowing Rhys had used his knowledge of Cal's feelings for him to manipulate who made love to whom on their first night together left Finn feeling cold and used. Yes, he'd enjoyed every second of burying himself inside of Rhys, but what if that memory would always be tainted by the knowledge that Rhys had orchestrated how things would play out?

Finn realized Dane was still waiting for an answer. He didn't know the man very well, but his instinct was that he could trust him. But as angry as he was at Cal, the secret Cal had kept for so long was his to tell, not Finn's. He ignored the voice in his head reminding him it was the same reason Rhys hadn't told him the truth.

"There's no future for me at the ranch," he said simply.

Dane studied him for a moment, then nodded in understanding. "What are your plans?" he asked.

An ache settled in Finn's chest at the realization that the future he'd longed for was at hand, but he dreaded taking that final step. "Um, there's a ranch hiring a couple towns over. Thought I'd check it out," he managed to get out before dropping his eyes back down to Emma who was starting to nod off as the bottle grew emptier.

"Well, if you have some time, I could use a hand around here," Dane remarked as he polished off the last of his pancakes and then reached for the baby.

Finn reluctantly handed her over, then tried to force the food into his mouth. He suspected Dane was throwing him a bone. "What do you need help with?" he asked.

"The guy that was supposed to tear down my barn and build me a new one flaked out on me. Said he's backed up with other jobs."

Finn froze at that and laid his fork down. "Someone from around here?" he asked, remembering the way Dane had fervently stood up for him in town.

Dane leaned back in his chair and began burping the baby. "Don't even give me that look, Finn. You even think about blaming yourself for this crap, I will put this baby down and kick your ass from here into the next county," he said firmly. "You really think I want to give my business to a guy who thinks he knows how I should live my life?"

Finn hadn't thought about it that way. He'd always been on the receiving end of being refused service so he hadn't considered it the other way around.

"I don't know anything about building a barn," Finn finally said.

"Well, luckily I do. I worked construction while I was putting myself through vet school so between the two of us I think we can figure it out. Soon as I find someone to keep any eye on this little girl here," Dane said as he brought the baby up to his face for a kiss, "we can get started. I've got an extra room if you need a place to stay," he offered casually.

Finn's throat refused to cooperate so he managed a nod, then took another stab at the food.

CHAPTER 13

*C*allan dismounted from his horse and led the animal into the barn and began stripping off the tack. He heard a car in the driveway and his heart stopped and he felt himself rushing to the door-way, hoping against hope that he'd see a blonde head in the passenger seat of whomever was bringing Finn home where he belonged. He'd known that Finn would be gone this morning, but hearing Rhys confirm it had been hard. Anything Finn could have carried, he'd taken, though he'd left the heavier items since he'd obviously walked to wherever he was going. Seeing that Finn hadn't even taken West had been another blow to Callan. He'd spent months picking out the perfect horse for Finn two years ago and Finn leaving the animal behind was a clear sign that Finn wanted no reminders of the man that had betrayed him.

The car that pulled up in front of the barn was a small, basic sedan and Callan only recognized the young woman once she climbed out of the car.

"Wendy," he said with surprise as the veterinary technician from Dr. Sanders' office walked up to the barn, her palms running nervously over her thighs.

"Hello, Mr. Bale." She nodded at him, then to someone behind him.

A quick glance over his shoulder proved that Rhys had appeared to cover him in case their visitor proved to be a threat.

"It's Callan," he said. "This is Rhys."

"Hi," she said shyly to Rhys, then turned her attention back to Callan. She was a pretty thing, petite with long brown hair and hazel eyes. He guessed her to be around Finn's age.

"What can I do for you?" he asked, hating that his suspicions instantly surfaced at her appearance.

Poor Wendy looked like she was going to break down in tears and Callan looked over at his shoulder at Rhys for help. Women and tears weren't his thing. And by the shaking of Rhys' head, he guessed they weren't his either.

"I owe you an apology for the way I behaved at the clinic the other day," she said as she tried to hold back her tears. "I became a vet tech so I could help animals and that calf needed me…" Wendy wiped her arm across her face. "I was a coward. I didn't want to lose my job-" she said sadly.

Callan felt sorry for her. "Wendy…"

But Wendy barreled on as if he hadn't interrupted. "If I could do it all over again, I would," she said passionately. "I'm sorry," she whispered.

"It's okay," he said. "The calf made it." A look of relief flashed over her, but then she shook her head.

"I quit right after you left. I got a job over at the drycleaner's till I can save up enough money to move to Missoula," she said in a rush. "Finn and I went to high school together – he was always real nice to me. I know the stuff Hunter said about him was a lie," she said in a strangled voice. "I tried to tell Doc Sanders and Anita that after Finn called looking for help for your calf. They said some awful stuff about him. I should've stuck up for him," she said, then started crying uncontrollably.

Callan pulled her into his arms and stroked her back as he felt her tears seep through his shirt. She finally quieted, then leaned back from him and laughed in embarrassment. "Sorry," she said as she looked at the wetness she'd left behind. An unexplainable emotion went through Callan and he felt himself softening.

"It's okay," he said as she stepped back. "Finn's actually not here."

"I know, I saw him on my way out here. He was helping Dr. Winters with his barn – tearing it down, I guess."

Callan glanced over his shoulder at Rhys who had stiffened at the news that Finn hadn't run as far as they thought.

"I stopped and talked to him. Told him how sorry I was for everything," she said as tears threatened again. Callan didn't even have a fucking tissue for her. Wendy solved the problem by wiping her face with her sleeve. "He said there was nothing to forgive."

That sounded exactly like something Finn would say.

"If that's what Finn said, then it must be true," Callan said.

Wendy laughed again, then started to go back to her car. She hesitated before turning around.

"Mr. Bale-"

"Callan," he reminded her gently.

"Callan, I was wondering if you might be able to help me with something. I mean, I know I don't really deserve it…"

"Of course, Wendy. What is it?" he interjected.

"I volunteer with an equine rescue group and we got a horse in a few weeks ago that was pretty badly treated. No one's been able to work with him and there's talk that he'll need to be put down," she began. "My daddy always told me you had a way with horses and my best friend Amy said you worked wonders with her horse before her parents made her move him…" Wendy's voice dropped off suddenly as she realized what she was saying. Amy's parents had been one of the first boarders to leave after Hunter's accusations.

"The answer is yes. I'll take a look at him,' he said.

Wendy smiled wide and suddenly threw herself into his arms. "Thank you, Mr. Bale. He's the most amazing horse and I know you'll be able to help him," she said quickly. "We can get him down here tomorrow if that will work for you," she said hopefully.

He nodded, got another hug for his efforts, then Wendy was waving and driving off, a trail of dust in her wake.

Arms closed around him from behind and a light kiss was pressed to his neck. The move should have had him looking all over the place to see if they were being watched, but instead he was turning in Rhys' arms and kissing him.

"You're such a good man, Callan Bale," Rhys said against his lips, then kissed him softly. Strong arms wrapped around his neck as Rhys hugged him and whispered, "I want to go and bring him home." His voice was vulnerable, shaky.

"Me too," Callan heard himself admitting. And it was true. He hadn't even realized when things had shifted and he'd decided he was going to try to make a life with Finn and Rhys in a town that didn't want them. Not to mention the father that would spew his unfiltered, cruel words as his disease continued to consume him.

Rhys released him and stepped back, then shuffled in front of him the way Finn always did when he was hiding something. "What?" Callan asked.

"Frank called. I have to go in to the local police department for a random drug screen this afternoon. It's part of the routine," he said quietly, the shame in his voice evident.

"Don't you fucking do that," Callan snapped as he grabbed Rhys by the arms. "Don't you act like you have something you should be ashamed of," he nearly yelled.

Rhys pulled free of him and Callan felt his emotional withdrawal as well. It was like being kicked in the ribs.

"Rhys-" he began.

"I need a ride to the police station," Rhys muttered.

Callan knew it was a fight he wouldn't win, so he nodded and said, "Let me put away my horse and then we can go."

~

*R*hys couldn't believe he'd forgotten why he was here. Less than two weeks in the middle of nowhere on a run-down ranch surrounded by dust and horse shit and already he was dreaming of mornings waking up with Finn and Callan wrapped around him after nights of endless fucking. Not once had he thought about the numerous plans he'd made for revenge on the former lover that had destroyed his life and ended four others. No, he'd been letting himself get wrapped up in a dream world that was just that – a fucking dream.

Finn was gone, Callan would never be free enough to be truly out and Rhys sure as hell didn't want to be sloppy seconds to either man. Sure, Callan had enjoyed fucking the hell out of him this morning, but that's all it was. Rhys should know better than anyone that a good, hard fuck was just that. It wasn't a license to give up everything he'd fought for these past two years.

"Stop it!" Callan snapped at him from the driver's seat.

"Stop what?" Rhys muttered.

"Stop questioning if what we have is real or not," Callan said as he steered the truck onto the main road.

"What we have?" Rhys forced himself to say with a laugh. "What we have is you giving good head and me liking a nice big dick in my ass," he bit out.

"Now who's the liar?" Callan said coldly.

Jesus, he couldn't take this. Rhys managed to keep his cool on the outside, but he felt his stomach rolling as the distance between himself and Callan grew. "I'll call Frank and ask him to find me something else." Rhys' heart broke when Callan didn't respond and the rest of the ride was made in silence.

Callan pulled to a stop in front of the police station, then got out of the truck. "You don't need to come with me," Rhys said, but Callan slammed the door closed and stalked to the entrance. Apparently Callan had decided to enjoy his complete humiliation, Rhys thought to himself as he climbed out of the truck and followed Callan into the station. *Fucking perfect.*

~

*C*allan seethed as he waited for Rhys to follow him. He had no doubt in his mind that Rhys was letting his embarrassment about his status as an ex-con cloud his thinking, but it still pissed him off as being referred to as just another good fuck.

Rhys elbowed past him and stepped up to a desk where a young deputy was sitting, his pimply face and crooked teeth pulling into a sneer when Rhys told him why he was there.

"Deputy Rollins, he's here," the guy shouted as his beady eyes stayed on Rhys. Callan had to give his lover credit because he stood there, back straight and tall as the kid tried to look down on him. But Callan didn't miss the slight tremor that went through Rhys' body as a second deputy appeared from the back.

"Afternoon, Mr. Tellar, what brings you in today?" Deputy Rollins asked, even though he clearly knew.

"Random drug screen," Rhys muttered, his eyes flicking briefly back to Callan.

"That's right," Rollins drawled as he pretended to look through some paperwork. "Heard you and Mr. Henry had a little run-in a while back. Said you threatened him," Rollins said casually.

"You gonna get on with it, Rollins?" Callan said from his position near the door. Apparently Dare's finest hadn't even noticed him standing near the door because he looked up in surprise. The guy might as well be drooling in his eagerness to provoke Rhys into action.

"Mr. Bale, how are you today? Heard you had some trouble with a cut fence in your south pasture last week."

"That's interesting that you say that, Deputy. I don't recall telling anyone my fence was cut."

The deputy stiffened and the younger officer paled. "Doc Sanders mentioned it," the younger one said.

Callan stepped up to the desk next to Rhys and softly said, "All we told Doc Sanders was that our calf was injured. We never told him how and he didn't examine him."

Rollins pulled himself up tall and said, "That other vet said something about it during his little coming out party at the hardware store." The deputy looked strangely proud of himself.

"Dr. Winters didn't say that the south pasture was the one vandal-ized," Rhys pointed out.

Both officers looked at each other, then Rollins crossed his arms and said, "Follow me, Mr. Tellar."

Rhys made a move to do as the deputy directed, but Callan grabbed him by the arm and said, "No."

Rollins looked positively giddy and said, "Mr. Tellar, failure to comply means immediate revocation of your parole."

"He'll take the test. But not here. Dr. Meyer's office is down the street."

"That's not protocol, Mr. Bale," Rollins said as he pulled out his handcuffs. Callan stepped in front of Rhys.

"You touch him and I will drop you like the piece of shit you are," Callan warned.

"Rollins, what's going on here?" came a voice from the back of the office. Both deputies immediately straightened and if Callan hadn't known better, he would have sworn they were preparing themselves to salute the older man as he moved into the room.

"Sheriff Granger, I didn't hear you come in," Rollins mumbled.

The sheriff looked to be in his late forties and moved with the ease and confidence that came from years of earning respect. "No doubt," the sheriff commented, apparently unsurprised that his deputies were so oblivious to their surroundings.

"Mr. Tellar was ordered to submit to a random drug screen as part of the terms of his parole, but he's refused," Rollins gushed as he motioned to Rhys.

"That's not what I heard, Rollins," the sheriff said. "I believe they asked for the test to be administered by a medical professional."

"It's against protocol," the younger deputy murmured, but then snapped his mouth shut when Granger's hard eyes shifted to him.

"If either of you had bothered to read the fucking protocol, you'd know that Mr. Tellar's request is appropriate." Both men shut up at the venom in their superior's tone. The sheriff turned to Rhys and Callan.

"Mr. Tellar, Mr. Bale, I'm Sheriff Bill Granger." They each shook the man's hand. "I apologize for my deputies here," Granger sneered as he cast the two officers another hard look. "I was voted into office a few weeks ago and inherited the prior sheriff's...leavings." The deputies flinched at the crude term, but remained silent. "Rollins, Hargrove, get your asses out on patrol, now!"

Both deputies stared mutinously at Callan and Rhys, then hurried out the back entrance.

"Mr. Bale, I understand you've had some issues with vandalism on your property in the past couple of years. Why don't we discuss that on the way to Dr. Meyer's clinic?"

～

*C*allan shook the sheriff's hand and watched him head back towards the police station. The man hadn't said much other than asking a lot of questions about the incidents that had plagued the ranch for the past two years, but Callan considered it small victory that the new sheriff had at least listened.

Anger and frustration rolled in his stomach as he watched Rhys sign some paperwork and head towards him. The man refused to get out of the funk he was in and it was pissing Callan off like nothing else. They left the clinic and began walking down the sidewalk to where the truck was parked. Rhys walked a step behind him and his shoulders were slumped, his eyes downcast. It was like all the fight had left him.

And Callan was fucking done.

"Fucking son of a bitch," he said, then grabbed Rhys by the collar of his shirt and slammed him back against the brick wall between the clinic and the hair salon next door. He ignored the women coming out of the salon and covered Rhys' mouth with his. A gasp sounded behind him, but he was more interested in the man struggling under his hold.

"Callan-" Rhys started to say, but Callan pressed the advantage and thrust his tongue past the other man's lips. Rhys tried to push him away for a few seconds before he finally submitted and relaxed in

Callan's grip and opened wider. Callan sucked Rhys' tongue into his own mouth and moaned when Rhys lovingly explored him.

"Oh my," they heard behind them and Callan finally released Rhys and prepared himself for the next battle. Two women with freshly done hairdos were watching them with their mouths hanging open. One was Mrs. Greene.

"You boys sure do know how to put on a show, Mr. Bale," Mrs. Greene said with a sly smile. "Evelyn, close your mouth, dear," she said to her companion. "You look like a fish." Callan felt Rhys stirring behind him. "I don't believe we've been introduced," she said as she reached her hand around Callan towards Rhys.

"Rhys Tellar," Rhys managed to get out, though he was still out of breath from their kiss.

"Harriet Greene," Mrs. Greene said. "This is Evelyn Turner."

Callan winced as he realized the other woman was a friend of Dolly's. So much for telling his aunt what he'd done before she heard it from someone else. Not that it mattered since several other people had been witness to his show of rebellion. Some looked flabbergasted, a few curious. Not that it mattered – he was just getting started.

"Would you excuse us, Mrs. Greene? Rhys and I have some errands to run."

"Of course, dear," she said with a knowing smile.

Callan grabbed Rhys' hand and dragged him down the sidewalk.

"What the fuck, Callan?" Rhys said in a low voice as he tried to tug his hand free. Callan came to a wrenching stop.

"You told me to fight for what I want so that's what I'm doing. Are you going to join me or are you going to keep pretending like what we have doesn't mean anything?" Callan felt Rhys' hand tighten in his and then that spark that was Rhys flared to life in his eyes.

"Lead the way," was all Rhys said.

CHAPTER 14

*R*hys didn't dare speak a word as Callan sped the truck down the county highway back towards the ranch. He wasn't sure what had lit a fire under the man's ass, but watching Callan demolish his way through town had been almost as much fun as getting his brains fucked out this morning. And it had started with the two pricks in uniform at the police station. They'd enjoyed knowing they had complete control over Rhys and there was not a fucking thing he could have done about it.

He hadn't initially noticed the men slip up in regards to knowing about the cut fence, but he was glad Callan had picked up on it because his chances of walking out of that police station with a drug test that hadn't been tampered with were zero to none. Those so called officers of the law had been looking for any excuse to put him behind bars and he shuddered to think how close they'd come to succeeding.

After kissing the shit out of him in front of God and everyone, Callan had proceeded to drag him to every establishment that had rejected Finn and tried to decimate Callan's business. He held Rhys' hand through the whole thing and had even kissed him on more than one occasion when he thought people might need a visual that Callan really was an out and proud, rainbow flag-carrying homo who'd managed to infiltrate their ranks for years. And thanks to Callan, Rhys had finally managed to get the cowboy hat he'd been wanting since the clerk at the feed store was too overcome with shock at seeing two men kissing in front of him to nix the purchase.

Rhys could tell something was still driving Callan and he guessed what it was. But it wasn't until Callan veered the truck onto the short, gravel driveway of Dane's property that he was sure and hope flared in him. Callan slammed on the brakes in front of the half torn down barn and two shirtless men looked up from their work. Rhys only had eyes for Finn as he climbed out of the truck and leaned back against the door to watch the show. Dane seemed to know something was up and stepped away from Finn.

"Cal?" Finn asked as Callan approached him. His eyes shot to Rhys in confusion, but before he could say anything Callan was on him and kissing the shit out of him. Rhys knew that kissing an angry Callan was like kissing a live wire so it was no surprise when Finn dropped the hammer he'd been holding and wrapped his arms around Callan. Lust sparked through Rhys at the sight and he hoped for one more miracle today.

Callan released Finn and stepped back. "I've done everything wrong, Finn. From day one. It was the only way I knew how to be with you and still be worthy of you. But I see now that I never really was."

Rhys stiffened when Callan pointed to him. "But he is. He has fought at your side from the day he came into our lives, Finn. Don't blame him for something I did. Don't punish him because I was weak."

Callan grabbed Finn by the neck. "I'm done standing in front of you instead of beside you and I'm done hiding behind promises I can't keep. I betrayed your trust, but if you let me, I'll spend the rest of my life trying to make it up to you. I love you and I want you to come home where you belong. But I love him too," Callan said, again looking at Rhys and Rhys felt his whole body go numb at the admission. "I won't choose between you so if you come home, you come home to both of us."

Rhys watched Callan kiss Finn again, this time soft and slow and deep and Rhys knew Callan was thinking it could be for the last time. Callan dropped his hands from Finn, spun on his heel and turned back towards the truck. He didn't go to the driver's side though. He stopped in front of Rhys and grabbed him the same way he had Finn. "I love you, Rhys, but I need you to decide if you want to go home to Chicago or if you're already home." Callan kissed him in the same, reverent way he'd kissed Finn, then let him go.

Rhys grabbed his arm before he could walk away. "Let's go home, Callan," he said simply and Callan's eyes softened and he nodded. "Love you," Rhys said as he gave Callan a quick kiss. As Callan walked around the truck to the driver's side, Rhys turned to look at Finn who was standing shell-shocked in the same exact spot Callan had left him in. It was too hard to say any words and Rhys knew if he touched Finn he might not be able to let him go, so he climbed up in the truck next to Callan and forced his eyes forward as Callan turned the truck around and headed home.

～

Three fucking days. Three days and not one word from Finn. "Rhys, do it somewhere else," Callan said from inside the arena. The white horse that the rescue group had dropped off a couple of days ago was pressed up against the wooden fence, trying to get as far away from Callan as he could. A myriad of scars ran the length of the animal's coat.

"Do what somewhere else?" Rhys muttered from where he stood leaning against the outside of the round enclosure.

"Have your little freak out moment. He can sense your anxiety," Callan said quietly as he patiently waited the horse out.

Callan was right of course, but he knew the other man wasn't as unaffected as he seemed. There was a weariness in Callan that hadn't been there before and his lovemaking every night was borderline frantic. Rhys knew it was because Callan was expecting him to walk away too - to make that phone call to Frank saying he needed a new job. But the instant Callan had told him he'd loved him, everything had changed for Rhys. He still had a few friends on the force so his plan was to keep pushing for the truth about Tom to come out, but he wasn't willing to throw away a life with Callan to satisfy his lust for vengeance. There would be a day when Tom double-crossed the wrong person and wouldn't be able to walk away from it.

"Rhys?"

Rhys realized he'd gotten lost in thought before responding to Callan and now the other man was watching him with concern. His stomach did a little flip-flop, but he waved Callan off and said, "I'm okay. I'll start bringing the horses in." Callan watched him a moment longer, then nodded and returned his attention back to the horse.

Twenty minutes later Rhys was helping Callan corral the horse into his stall. Since the animal hated being touched, Callan had set a couple of stock guard gates between the barn and the arena to allow the horse to make his way into the barn on his own. The barriers kept the animal from taking off, but meant that Callan didn't have to traumatize the horse by roping him or using crueler methods to control the animal.

"Slow going," Rhys said as Callan slid the stall door closed and watched the animal pace back and forth in agitation.

"Someone really did a number on him," Callan said sadly. Before Rhys could say anything else or do what he really wanted to do which was kiss the shit out of Callan, a car approached and they both tensed and hurried to the barn door.

"Fuck," Rhys said softly when he recognized Wendy's little sedan rolling up and the disappointment flooded through him.

Callan grabbed him by the shoulder. "It was a lot to ask of him, Rhys. Maybe too much," he sighed. "But you could still try…maybe you guys could-"

"If you finish that sentence I swear I will beat the ever loving shit out of you!" Rhys nearly snarled as he grabbed Callan's neck. "He's going to come home," Rhys whispered, then ghosted a kiss over Callan's lips. "And we're going to figure out how to make this work." Callan grabbed his wrist and nodded, then kissed him back.

"Um, Mr. Bale?" Wendy said with a cough.

Rhys smothered a laugh as he realized he and Callan had completely forgotten about Wendy's arrival. They both turned to see her shifting nervously behind them, a blush on her cheeks.

"Sorry Wendy," Rhys started to say, but Wendy cut him off.

"Are you kidding me? That was so hot!" The second the words were out of her mouth she slapped a hand over it as she realized what she'd said. "Oh my God," she stuttered and Callan and Rhys both laughed as she closed her eyes in embarrassment. "I brought King some carrots," she choked out as she held up the carrots as if to prove why she was there.

"He's in his stall," Callan said with a chuckle as Wendy darted past him. "We'll be up at the house if you need anything," he called over his shoulder.

"Okay," came the response.

Rhys let Callan take his hand as they headed to the house Rhys had essentially moved into. Once Finn came back it would be tight quarters in the small foreman's house, but Rhys could only see that as being a good thing.

"How's your dad today?" he asked Callan.

Callan's hand tightened in his. "Same. Didn't recognize me at all." Rhys knew it was a painful topic for Callan and didn't press him.

"My turn to cook, right?" Rhys began to say, then let his words fall off when they heard the sound of another car coming up the road. They were closer to Callan's house than to the barn and whoever was driving the shiny, black luxury car seemed to notice because the car bypassed the barn and pulled to a stop near them. They both tensed, but Callan refused to release his hand when Rhys tried to step in front of him.

The door opened and a tall, well-built man with thick, slightly too long, coal black hair got out. If the car didn't already signify this guy was from out of town, his black, sleek slacks and crisp white dress shirt did for sure. Black sunglasses hid his eyes, but the only thing that had Rhys' full attention was the shoulder holster the guy was wearing over his shirt, putting the two black Glock pistols he had on him within easy reach.

"Hotter than hell out here," the guy muttered as he began rolling up the sleeves of his shirt to reveal tanned, muscular forearms. The sunglasses came off and if Rhys hadn't been on high alert, he would have taken the time to admire how good looking the man was.

"Can we help you?" he heard Callan say, the stiffness in his voice clear. Fear went through Rhys as he realized he and Callan had no way to defend themselves. The only weapon on the property was the rifle Callan used when he went out to check the fences and that was locked up in the tack room in the barn.

"I'm here to have a little word with Mr. Tellar." The tone was casual, but the man's predatory stance and shifting eyes made it clear this was not a man to fuck with or underestimate. Rhys ripped his hand free of Callan and stepped away from him. If this guy was coming after him, he sure as hell wasn't going to let Callan be in the line of fire.

The man appeared to notice the move, but didn't react. He also didn't respond when Callan stepped back to Rhys' side and grabbed his hand again.

"You can relax Mr. Bale, I'm just here to talk to him," the guy said finally with a sigh.

"So talk," Callan responded crisply.

"Mr. Tellar, my name is Jaxon Reid. Ben Reid was my brother."

~

*C*allan heard Rhys suck in a sharp breath and he turned to see that his lover had gone pale at the name.

"Rhys," Callan said, jerking on Rhys' hand to get his attention. He needed to know if this stranger was a threat to them and right now he was completely clueless. Rhys clearly had some association to him, but the guns the man was sporting like they were an extension of his body weren't reassuring. Rhys didn't answer him. He just continued to stare at the other man, completely at a loss for words.

"Rhys!" Callan said sharply and Rhys finally turned to look at him.

"Ben Reid was one of the men on the protective detail for my CI," Rhys managed to get out.

Callan stiffened as he remembered the story Rhys had shared with him just a couple of nights ago. Frank hadn't gone into details about Rhys' past when he'd asked Callan to take him on and Callan hadn't wanted to press Rhys to talk about it before he was ready. They'd only discussed it the other night because Rhys had mentioned wanting to return to Chicago after his parole ended so he could try to make some headway on the case that had sent him to prison. The case that had cost the man in front of them his brother.

"Mr. Reid," Rhys started to say, but then stopped, unable to get anything else out.

Angry at seeing the man he loved being put through this, Callan did what his instincts had been telling him to from the moment the car pulled up and pushed Rhys behind him. "I'm sorry for your loss, Mr. Reid, but Rhys isn't responsible."

"Yes, I am," Rhys said softly. "It's my fault."

"Rhys," Callan started, but Rhys put a hand on his arm and then moved past him to stand in front of the still quiet Jaxon Reid.

"I trusted someone I shouldn't have and it cost your brother his life. I'm sorry. If I could change it, I would. I didn't know Ben very well, but he seemed like a really good man." Callan hated hearing the pain radiate through Rhys' voice and he hated the man standing across from him even more because the fucker hadn't said one word while he stood there, his arms folded insolently as he looked down on Rhys as if standing in judgement of him.

Callan started to step forward with the intent to physically get this man off his land, but he must have sensed that was the case because he put his hand up and said, "Take it easy, Mr. Bale. As I said before, I'm only here to talk." His eyes focused on Rhys.

"Tom Rawlings is dead," Jaxon announced without reservation, his tone flat.

*R*hys shook his head in disbelief, but couldn't find the words to ask the obvious question.

"How?" Callan asked for him.

"ME's report says self-inflicted gunshot wound," Jaxon said.

"Bullshit," Rhys heard himself saying. "Fucker was too in love with himself to blow his brains out."

"I said that was what was in the ME's report," Jaxon said with the faintest hint of a smile. A chill went through Rhys as he realized what the man wasn't saying. Jesus, was he standing in front of the man who'd done what Rhys had dreamed of doing for so long?

"Was it you?" Rhys asked without preamble.

Jaxon studied him for a long time, then turned and opened his car door. He handed Rhys a manila envelope. "Give that to your attorney."

"What is it?" Rhys asked as he opened the envelope, though he didn't need an answer once he saw what was on the pages that spilled out into his hand. A CD slipped out too.

"Rhys?" Callan asked as he examined the pages.

"Money transfers, transcripts of wire taps, surveillance," Rhys said in awe as he flipped through the pages. He stopped when he saw his name on one of the transcripts. "They caught him on tape admitting to stealing the location of the safe house from me," he whispered as the truth hit him. Was it really going to be this easy? He looked up at Jaxon. "How did you get this?"

The man again evaded his question and said, "The DA that prosecuted you has already started the processing of having the charges dismissed, but you should still have an attorney take a look at those. I think you're looking at a pretty hefty settlement from the city of Chicago. They're not going to like having to explain to the public why they sent an innocent cop to jail."

Rhys looked up at Callan and smiled. "It's over, Callan. It's really over." An overwhelming sense of relief flooded through his body as Callan pulled him into his arms. He didn't give a shit that the other man was watching as he kissed Callan hard.

The sound of several neighing horses had Callan tensing in his arms, then suddenly releasing him as the noise from the barn grew. Callan was already running toward the barn when the scent of smoke filled Rhys' nostrils. "Oh God," he said as he took off after Callan.

"Wendy!" he heard Callan shout as he neared the barn. Black smoke started to billow between the slats of the wooden roof as the sound of panicked horses filled the air. Rhys' heart stopped as Callan raced into the barn. He felt Jaxon right on his heels and they both reached the building just as flames began ripping through the ceiling. The hayloft.

"Callan!" Rhys shouted as he tried to see through the thick, black smoke that was drifting down from the ceiling.

"I've got her!" Callan shouted and Rhys felt a punch of relief as Callan carried Wendy past him. Blood trickled from an injury on her forehead.

The sound of terrified horses over the roar of flames had Rhys racing into the barn. He heard Callan screaming his name, but ignored him and tore open the first stall door. West flew past him the second he opened the door and he saw that Jaxon had managed to free Kirby from the opposite stall. Getting Callan's gelding and two more horses out took only seconds, but the rescue horse clung to the back of its stall and refused to budge. Rhys' eyes burned as he shouted at the horse, but it just reared up and slammed its body into the back of the stall as if trying to break through it. Flames rolled over his head and he heard wood cracking as the support beams started to weaken. He guessed that he had less than a minute before the roof came crashing down.

"Rhys! We have to get out now!" Jaxon shouted from somewhere on the other side of the barn. Rhys glanced at the barn doors which were both nearly obliterated from the black cloud of smoke that plunged the barn into darkness. Decision made, Rhys rushed into the stall and waved his arms at the huge horse. The panicked animal lunged at him, then slammed into him with its huge body as it raced past him. He hit the floor hard and sucked in a mouthful of smoke, then started choking.

"Rhys!"

"Here!" he shouted, then strong arms were lifting him. Callan.

He felt himself being half lifted, half dragged as another set of hands grabbed him and Callan and Jaxon pulled him out the door. The oxygen burned his lungs as it mixed with smoke.

"Jesus," Callan said as he clung to Rhys. "You fucking son of a bitch!" he snarled as he clutched Rhys to him. Then his voice softened, the words so quiet among the popping, crackling sounds of the fire that Rhys barely heard them. "God, I thought I'd lost you."

∼

*C*allan couldn't hold on to Rhys tight enough. He'd watched as horse after horse had come flying through the doors, but no Rhys. Jaxon had managed to get out, but hadn't hesitated to go back in with Callan when they realized Rhys was still in the burning building. Pieces of the roof had started to fall around them as embers rained down on their shoulders and lit up the hay that was strewn around the aisle and stalls. They'd managed to get Rhys to his feet, but the back door was engulfed in flames so they'd had to work their way back to the front of the barn.

"I'm okay," he heard Rhys say against his chest, his voice hoarse from the smoke. "Is Wendy okay?" he asked.

"Callan!" he heard Jaxon calling out to him. The man was kneeling next to Wendy, examining the gash on her head. "She's waking up."

Callan helped Rhys to his feet and then hurried over to Wendy's side. "Wendy, honey, can you hear me?"

The sound of an approaching vehicle had them all looking up as a black SUV tore up the driveway. It screeched to a stop at the point where the driveway widened. Dane climbed out of the driver's side and hurried around the front, a black bag in his hand. He ran straight for Wendy.

Finn clamored out of the passenger side, his wide eyes taking in the barn, then finally finding them and Callan saw the relief flood through him.

"Finn, can you get Emma?" Dane shouted and Callan could see Finn was torn between getting to their sides and getting the baby.

"We're okay, Finn!" Callan yelled, then nodded. Finn hesitated, then opened the backseat of the SUV.

"What happened?" Dane asked as he dropped to his knees next to Wendy. The young woman was waking up but seemed groggy at first. Suddenly she struggled against Dane as he examined her injury.

"Men! There were two men in the barn!" she said in a rush. "I heard them in the hayloft. I started to climb the ladder and then they came down and they hit me and I fell-"

"Shhh, it's okay Wendy," Callan said just before a gunshot shattered the air around them.

"Finn!" Callan heard Rhys shout and he turned just in time to see someone jump into to the passenger seat of Dane's SUV. Finn lay crumpled in the dirt, blood staining his chest. The SUV roared to life and leapt forward.

"Finn!" Callan screamed as he began running, his heart in his throat as he realized Finn wasn't moving.

"Emma!" Dane suddenly shouted from behind him and Callan realized the baby was still in the car. He made a grab for the door handle as the SUV barreled past him as it was turning in the driveway, but the impact knocked him to the ground.

"Rhys," he heard Jaxon say calmly as the man stood and pulled both guns from his holster and handed one to Rhys. "Back tires," he said simply, then raised the gun. The driver of the SUV had managed to get the vehicle turned around and was picking up speed as both Jaxon and Rhys took aim and fired simultaneously. Two loud claps reverberated through the air as the back tires blew out. The vehicle swerved but stayed upright as it veered off the road and came to a jerky halt in the pasture.

Callan ran to Finn and dropped down next to him. "Finn," he shouted as he shook him hard, then felt for a pulse.

"Emma!" he heard Dane screaming again and saw Jaxon push the vet back and shout at him to stay put. Rhys was already running towards the passenger side of the SUV where the baby's car seat was.

Jaxon was approaching the driver's side. Jaxon fired two shots into the driver's side window, shattering the glass with the first bullet, hitting the driver with the second.

"Clear!" Jaxon shouted.

"Clear!" he heard Rhys shout and saw that Rhys had yanked the passenger from the SUV and thrown him to the ground. The man was screaming in fear with his hands above his head.

Callan looked down at Finn and shouted for Dane. The vet looked at him, then the SUV, clearly torn.

"She's good!" Jaxon shouted as he opened the back door. "She's safe!" he said, his eyes on Dane. Callan saw relief go through Dane, then he was running towards him and Finn.

"Get his shirt open!" he yelled as he began checking Finn's vitals. Callan tore his shirt open and froze at the sight of the blood drenching his chest. Rhys dropped down beside him, his hands reaching for Finn's.

"Jesus," he heard Rhys whisper. Rhys' hand closed around his upper arm hard as if looking for an answer that Callan didn't have.

"Breathing's labored, but good. Pulse is strong," Dane murmured as his fingers worked their way over Finn. "Finn, can you hear me?" he said as he pushed the shirt off Finn's shoulders to reveal a gaping wound just under his collar bone.

"Help me lift him," he said to Callan and Rhys and they both carefully leaned Finn forward.

"Through and through, that's good," Dane said as they lowered Finn back down.

"Callan!" he heard his aunt screaming and looked up to see her running down the driveway from the main house. "Oh my good Lord," she said as she saw Finn. "I called for help!"

"Cal?"

Everyone snapped their eyes down to Finn whose eyes fluttered open, then closed again as pain lanced through his features.

"Finn, baby, open your eyes," Rhys pleaded as his fingers skimmed over Finn's cheeks.

"Finn, talk to us," Callan whispered.

"Coming home…saw smoke," he managed to say as his eyes finally opened again and focused on them. "Emma!" he said suddenly and tried to lurch up.

"She's safe," Dane said as he glanced up to check on Jaxon who was carefully holding the baby against his chest as he kept his gun trained on the man lying cowering in the dry grass.

"I'm sorry, Dane. I didn't see them. I tried to get her!"

"It's okay, Finn. She's okay," Dane said as he reached into his bag and pulled out some gauze and pressed it to Finn's wound. "Hold that there," he said to Callan.

"Aunt Dolly, can you go check on Wendy?" Callan asked as he motioned to the young woman who was sitting on the edge of the driveway, her hand cradling her head.

"Of course," Dolly said as she hurried away.

"Who were they?" Finn asked as his eyes drifted to the barn as it began to buckle in on itself as the flames consumed it.

"Deputies Rollins and Hargove," Rhys said angrily. "Rollins is dead."

Callan felt rage consume him and he actually started to stand before Rhys grabbed his hand. "Callan, don't. It's over." Rhys was right, but the need to wrap his hands around the scrawny deputy's neck and wring the life out of him had him shaking. Callan felt Finn grab his hand and he instantly redirected all his attention to the younger man.

"Cal, I'm home on one condition," Finn said quietly, the word "home" taking away all the fury he was feeling and replacing it with hope.

"Anything," he said as he leaned down so he could hear Finn better.

"We need to get a bigger bed. You guys take up a lot of fucking room."

CHAPTER 15

allan stared at the charred ruins in silence as soft footsteps came up behind him. He turned to see his aunt approaching. She came to a stop next to him and wrapped an arm around his waist.

"You can rebuild it, darling," she said softly as he draped his arm around her shoulder.

"I can't do it anymore," he said quietly. "They're just going to keep coming for us."

His aunt patted his back softly. "This town's been asleep a long time, Callan. They're just starting to wake up. Give them a chance to finish opening their eyes before you make any big decisions."

Callan wasn't so sure. The one thing he was sure of was that he wasn't going to risk the men he loved again. His eyes drifted to where Rhys was moving Finn's stuff from his house to Callan's – well, their house now. He'd ordered the king sized bed he'd promised Finn this morning, though he wasn't sure how the hell they were going to get it in their room. Their room - God, he liked the sound of that.

"How would you feel about moving somewhere else?" he asked Dolly as he turned to face her. "We might be able to get enough for this place to start over."

"Unless starting over is in Boca Raton, count me out," she said with a sly smile as she handed him a sheaf of papers he hadn't noticed her carrying.

"What is this?" he asked as he skimmed it.

"It's a transfer for Power of Attorney. It gives me the right to make all decisions for your father's care and finances. I want you to sign it," she said as she produced a pen.

"I don't understand," he said, completely lost.

"It's time for you to let him go, Callan. He needs more than either you or I can give him."

Callan flinched as he realized what she was saying. "You want to put him in a home?"

"It's a place that helps people like him live as independently as they can," she countered. "I'm going to be nearby, Callan. I'll see him every day."

"Where?" he said.

"I already told you. Boca."

"Florida?" He couldn't believe this. "You want to move to Florida?"

"You remember your Uncle Stan's sister, Regina?" He did, but barely. Dolly's husband's side of the family had lived in California and he'd only met them a few times before Stan died and Dolly had moved to Montana to care for his father.

"She lost her husband a few months ago and has asked me to come stay with her for a while. The place your father would be living is only five minutes away and Regina's daughter runs it."

"Aunt Dolly, I can help out more," he began.

Dolly reached up to grab him by the face. "You listen to me, Callan Bale. This has nothing to do with that and you know it. You're a good man and you've made your mama proud with how well you've watched out for your father. Carter couldn't have asked for a better son than if he'd been standing in front of God when he did it."

Callan felt tears sting his eyes. "I don't want to lose you too," he admitted.

"Oh my boy," she cried as she hugged him. "You won't." She pushed back from him and said, "Build a life with your men" as she glanced over at the house. "Whether it's here or someplace else. As long as you're together, you'll always be home." Callan squeezed her until she squeaked, then she held out the pen expectantly. His hand shook as he signed, but in his heart he knew it was the right thing.

"Now give me a dollar," she said as she took the pen and papers back, then held out her hand.

Since arguing with Dolly rarely worked out well for him, he fished a dollar from his wallet and handed it to her. "Congratulations, you just bought yourself a ranch," she said. "I've got some cookies cooling up at the house. Finn's favorite," she called over her shoulder as she waved to Rhys as she walked past their house and began the trek back up the driveway.

He looked back at the burned out barn, then headed for the house. His family had some decisions to make.

~

"Careful with that."

Rhys cast a dark look at Finn as he sat comfortably in the porch swing while Rhys carried Finn's hulking TV into the house. He dropped the thing on the kitchen table, then grabbed a couple bottles of water from the fridge and went back outside to sit next to Finn.

"Why do you need the damn thing?" he muttered as he handed one of the bottles to Finn and took a long drink from his own. "Callan's already got a TV that was actually built in this decade."

"Thought it might be nice to have a TV in the bedroom," Finn said with a shrug, wincing slightly as he jolted the arm that was still in a sling.

Rhys reached down and let his lips hover over Finn's. "Baby, I can guarantee you that you are never going to have time to watch that TV while you're in bed." He covered Finn's mouth with his and groaned when Finn instantly opened for him. It had been too fucking long. Less than twenty-fours ago he'd nearly lost all of this.

Finn moaned and Rhys felt an arm lock around his neck. But then Finn grunted in pain and Rhys pulled back. He dropped his forehead against Finn's. "I suppose maybe you will be able to watch TV in bed for a while. At least till that comes off," he said as he glanced at the sling.

"Or I could watch you and Cal instead," Finn suggested.

Rhys' body responded instantly to the other man's comment and a whole slideshow of images flashed through his mind. The sound of boots on the porch stairs was a blessed distraction. He leaned back against the swing and put his arm around Finn's shoulders, careful not to touch his injury.

"You okay?" he asked Callan as the other man leaned across from them against the porch railing. Rhys handed him his water. It had been a long twenty-four hours since the fire and shooting. Rhys had spent much of it at the hospital with Finn who'd been admitted for observation, along with Wendy who'd ended up with a concussion while Callan had stayed at the ranch to wrangle up the horses that had scattered all over the property.

Sheriff Granger had arrived within a matter of hours to question Rhys about Rollins and Hargrove, who it turned out had been fired after the incident with his drug screening at the station. Rhys had felt sorry for the sheriff who was clearly wracked with guilt that the men had come after them as a result. Hargrove had admitted that he and Rollins had been the ones cutting fences and even poisoning the water supply that had killed so many of Callan's herd. Although it had been Rollins who'd shot Finn, it was Hargrove alone who would be spending the foreseeable future behind bars. Jaxon's bullet to Rollins' brain had seen to that.

"Dolly's taking my father to Florida. She found a place that can take care of him and she's going to move in with her sister-in-law. The ranch is ours," he said.

Finn stood and put his arms around Callan. "I'm sorry, Cal. I know how much she means to you." Callan held Finn close and dropped his chin on the other man's head.

"We need to make a decision about what to do with the place," Callan said. "We're not going to hide, but I don't want us to keep having to look over our shoulders either."

Rhys remained silent as did Finn.

"We could leave," Callan said. "Go someplace where people don't give a shit about what we are to each other."

"Is there such a place?" Rhys asked.

Callan stroked his hand up and down Finn's back as he fell quiet. Rhys wanted to laugh at how things had changed since his first day when he'd arrived at the ranch. He'd hated everything about the place the second he'd set foot on it, but now he couldn't imagine a life anywhere else. He looked up to make sure he had Callan's attention. "Callan, we'll follow you anywhere, but this is your home."

Callan shook his head. "This is just a place. My home is with you."

~

Finn closed his eyes as Cal's fingers kept moving up and down his back. The pain pills the doctor had prescribed for him had taken the edge off, but they had nothing on what Rhys and Cal were making him feel. Had it really only been three days since Cal stalked onto Dane's property, kissed the shit out of him and then told him he loved him and Rhys too? Part of him had wanted to run after the truck as it sped away that day, but the effect of Cal's betrayal had lingered and he'd spent three days torturing himself both for wondering if he should take the men back and waiting so damn long to do it.

Dane had stood quietly in the wings as Finn waffled back and forth, but the instant he said he was ready to go home, Dane had packed up Emma within minutes and they'd been on their way. It had been Dane who noticed the cloud of smoke first and by the time they reached the barn, a wall of orange flame had been shooting high into the sky. The fear that had overcome him at not knowing the fate of his men had been amplified by the undeniable regret that he'd waited too long. The sight of Rhys and Cal alive and well had stolen the breath from him and he'd actually struggled with Dane's request to get Emma out of the car, his need to touch his men that strong. After that there had been an explosion of sound and searing pain as he was hurtled backwards into the dirt. Then everything had gone dark.

"You okay?" Cal asked him and Finn knew the other man must have felt the shudder that had run through him. He nodded. "What do you think we should do?" Cal asked him.

Finn reveled at the way Cal said "we." He sighed and pulled back from Cal, then kissed him. "I love you," he said. Cal smiled and a look of peace came over him that Finn hadn't seen since the night the three of them had made love. "Rhys?" he said as he dropped his head back against Cal's chest, his body suddenly feeling weary as the pain medication began to draw him further under.

"Yeah, baby?" Rhys said, his big body settling at Finn's back, enveloping him in warmth.

"I love you."

"I know. I love you too." Lips caressed his temple as a set of hands closed around his waist. "Why don't you go lay down for a bit?" Rhys murmured in his ear.

Finn was about to say yes when his eyes caught on something on the horizon. Vehicle after vehicle was headed up the driveway. Finn smiled as he realized what he was seeing. "I can't. We have guests," he said softly.

"What the hell?" he heard Rhys say behind him. Cal shifted to look over his shoulder, but didn't release Finn, obviously not caring who saw the three of them wrapped around one another.

Truck after truck laden with lumber pulled up in front of the scorched pile of wood where the barn had sat. Finn saw Wendy climb out of her little sedan along with several other people and she waved at him. Sheriff Granger's patrol car pulled up and the man, dressed in everyday clothes, got out and started directing people. Mrs. Greene appeared and began arguing with the sheriff.

A black sedan trailed at the end of the caravan and Finn saw Dane get out and pull Emma out of the back seat. He recognized the guy with Dane as Jaxon Reid and the heated look that passed between the two men made Finn wonder what was going on with his new friend and the mysterious man who'd given Rhys his freedom back.

"It's a barn raising party," Cal said in disbelief.

"A what?" Rhys asked.

Finn pulled back from Cal and smiled as he watched the crowd of people start throwing debris into a huge trailer attached to a pick-up truck. "They're rebuilding our barn," Finn said. He looked up at Cal and Rhys who were both standing in stunned silence at the sight. He stepped past them and said, "Come on, let's go welcome our neighbors."

Cal and Rhys caught up to him by the time he reached the bottom of the porch stairs and he smiled when Cal's fingers twined with his and Rhys' arm carefully settled around his shoulders. It felt good to finally be home.

The End

ABOUT THE AUTHOR

Dear Reader,

I hope you enjoyed Rhys, Callan and Finn's story. They'll be back in Dane and Jax's story.

    As an independent author, I am always grateful for feedback so if you have the time and desire, please leave a review, good or bad, so I can continue to find out what my readers like and don't like. You can also send me feedback via email at sloane@sloanekennedy.com

Join my Facebook Fan Group: Sloane's Secret Sinners

Connect with me:
www.sloanekennedy.com
sloane@sloanekennedy.com

ALSO BY SLOANE KENNEDY

(Note: Not all titles will be available on all retail sites)

The Escort Series
Gabriel's Rule (M/F)

Shane's Fall (M/F)

Logan's Need (M/M)

Barretti Security Series
Loving Vin (M/F)

Redeeming Rafe (M/M)

Saving Ren (M/M/M)

Freeing Zane (M/M)

Finding Series
Finding Home (M/M/M)

Finding Trust (M/M)

Finding Peace (M/M)

Finding Forgiveness (M/M)

Finding Hope (M/M/M)

The Protectors
Absolution (M/M/M)

Salvation (M/M)

Retribution (M/M)

Forsaken (M/M)

Vengeance (M/M/M)

A Protectors Family Christmas

Atonement (M/M)

Revelation (M/M)

Redemption (M/M)

Non-Series

Letting Go (M/F)

15438518R00091

Printed in Germany
by Amazon
Distribution